PENGUIN BOOKS

The Pearl

Born in Salinas, California, in 1902, John Steinbeck grew up in a fertile agricultural valley about twenty-five miles from the Pacific Coast – and both valley and coast would serve as settings for some of his best fiction. In 1919 he went to Stanford University, where he intermittently enrolled in literature and writing courses until he left in 1925 without taking a degree. During the next five years he supported himself as a labourer and journalist in New York City, all the time working on his first novel, *Cup of Gold* (1929). After marriage and a move to Pacific Grove, he published two Californian fictions, *The Pastures of Heaven* (1932) and *To a God Unknown* (1933), and worked on short stories later collected in *The Long Valley* (1938). Popular success and financial security came only with *Tortilla Flat* (1935), stories about Monterey's paisanos. A ceaseless experimenter throughout his career, Steinbeck changed course regularly. Three powerful novels of the late 1930s focused on the Californian labouring class: *In Dubious Battle* (1936), *Of Mice and Men* (1937) and the book considered by many his finest, *The Grapes of Wrath* (1939). Early in the 1940s, Steinbeck became a filmmaker with *The Forgotten Village* (1941) and a serious student of marine biology with *Sea of Cortez* (1941). He devoted his services to the war, writing *Bombs Away* (1942) and the controversial play-novelette *The Moon is Down* (1942). *Cannery Row* (1945), *The Wayward Bus* (1947), *The Pearl* (1947), *A Russian Journal* (1948), another experimental drama, *Burning Bright* (1950), and *The Log from the Sea of Cortez* (1951) preceded publication of the monumental *East of Eden* (1952), an ambitious saga of the Salinas Valley and his own family's history. The last decades of his life were spent in New York City and Sag Harbor with his third wife, with whom he travelled widely. Later books include *Sweet Thursday* (1954), *The Short Reign of Pippin IV: A Fabrication* (1957), *Once There Was a War* (1958), *The Winter of Our Discontent* (1961), *Travels with Charley in Search of America* (1962), *America and Americans* (1966) and the posthumously published *Journal of a Novel: The 'East of Eden' Letters* (1969), *Viva Zapata!* (1975), *The Acts of King Arthur and His Noble Knights*

(1976) and *Working Days: The Journals of 'The Grapes of Wrath'* (1989). He died in 1968, having won a Nobel Prize in 1962.

Linda Wagner-Martin is Hanes Professor of English and Comparative Literature at the University of North Carolina, Chapel Hill, where she teaches modern and contemporary American literature, women's studies, and courses in biography and autobiography. Among her recent books are *Telling Women's Lives: The New Biography* (1994), *The Modern American Novel* (1989) and *Sylvia Plath: A Biography* (1987). She is co-editor of *The Oxford Companion to Women's Writing in the United States* and its companion anthology of women's writing.

JOHN STEINBECK

The Pearl

With an Introduction by Linda Wagner-Martin

Drawings by José Clemente Orozco

PENGUIN BOOKS

PENGUIN BOOKS

Published by the Penguin Group
Penguin Books Ltd, 80 Strand, London WC2R 0RL, England
Penguin Putnam Inc., 375 Hudson Street, New York, New York 10014, USA
Penguin Books Australia Ltd, 250 Camberwell Road, Camberwell, Victoria 3124, Australia
Penguin Books Canada Ltd, 10 Alcorn Avenue, Toronto, Ontario, Canada M4V 3B2
Penguin Books India (P) Ltd, 11 Community Centre, Panchsheel Park, New Delhi – 110 017, India
Penguin Books (NZ) Ltd, Cnr Rosedale and Airborne Roads, Albany, Auckland, New Zealand
Penguin Books (South Africa) (Pty) Ltd, 24 Sturdee Avenue, Rosebank 2196, South Africa

Penguin Books Ltd, Registered Offices: 80 Strand, London WC2R 0RL, England

www.penguin.com

First published in the USA by The Viking Press, 1947
First published in Great Britain by William Heinemann Ltd 1948
Published with *The Red Pony* in a Viking Compass edition 1965
Published in Penguin Books 1976
The Pearl published in Penguin Books 1993
This edition published in the USA in Penguin Books 1994
Published in Great Britain in Penguin Classics 2000

11

Copyright 1945 by John Steinbeck
Copyright renewed Elaine Steinbeck, John Steinbeck IV and Thom Steinbeck, 1973
Introduction copyright © Linda Wagner-Martin, 1994
All rights reserved

Introduction originally published in *Woman's Home Companion*
as 'The Pearl of the World'
Drawings by José Clemente Orozco

The moral right of the author of the introduction and of the illustrator
has been asserted

Set in 10.75/14 pt Monotype New Caledonia
Typeset by Rowland Phototypesetting Ltd, Bury St Edmunds, Suffolk
Printed in England by Clays Ltd, St Ives plc

Contents

Introduction

In 1939, John Steinbeck—who was considered a radical California writer, best known at the time for *In Dubious Battle*, his 1936 novel about unions and strike activity—found himself on the cover of *Time Magazine*. His new novel, *The Grapes of Wrath*, was a runaway success, making him the target for hate mail and FBI scrutiny, as well as commercial fame. In this long narrative about the dispossessed Okies (farmers from Oklahoma, devastated by years of drought on land that was a part of the so-called Dust Bowl) who traveled to California in search of any kind of work on profitable farms, Steinbeck seemed again to sympathize with collective strategies, to hint that communist cooperation was the way to settle economic inequities in the United States. Besides being a best-seller, *The Grapes of Wrath* won the Pulitzer Prize for fiction in 1940. And it was quickly made into a film starring Henry Fonda as Tom Joad, a film that many viewers found objectionable (it was the first American-made movie to show a pregnant woman on camera, for example; and it was assuredly and consistently about poor people, those whose lifestyles were so primitive that Americans with enough money for movie tickets did not like to be reminded that fellow citizens lived this way).

Steinbeck would have enjoyed the fame and money that his fiction brought him, but the persecution that resulted from his writing about the poor, people marginalized by the changing industrial patterns of the times, frightened him. The modest and soft-spoken Steinbeck, who had spent years and considerable personal energy studying ocean ecology, had trouble defining himself as a subversive, an unpatriotic man who was a threat to the national interest. Seemingly at the top of his profession with the appearance of *The Grapes of Wrath*, Steinbeck instead found himself going through torturous self-assessment.

By 1944–1945, when he wrote his novella *The Pearl*, he had pretty much decided that his view of himself was more credible than the versions the media, or the FBI, had created. But these years of personal questioning, and personal quest, had caused Steinbeck to come to terms with what wealth meant, with what an obsession with wealth (and in his case, perhaps, fame) could do to a community, as well as to the identity of the person experiencing that wealth and fame. As he had done before, he drew his personal convictions into the frame of the story he was writing, and when he chose the title for *The Pearl*, he intended readers to recall the biblical "pearl of great price." In that parable, the jewel for which the merchant trades everything he owns becomes the metaphor for Heaven. Everything in a person's earthly existence is worthless when compared with the joys of living with the Eternal Father in His Kingdom, or so the gospel of Matthew states.

In Steinbeck's parable, however, when "the great pearl, perfect as the moon . . . as large as a sea-gull's egg," is found by the illiterate and innocent Mexican man Kino, his discovery became a way for Steinbeck to assess the

American dream and to find it wanting. To become successful, to gain possessions and prominence, to become a force within a community—these were aspects of the dream that everyone recognized and few questioned. But for Steinbeck, the great notoriety of *The Grapes of Wrath* had been traumatic. After its publication, he turned inward and interrogated the values he had assumed he shared with most Americans. As a result of his experience, he saw that the established people in communities cared little about anyone else's misfortunes but would do whatever they could to keep prestige and position for themselves. The lives of the simple Kino and his wife, Juana, illustrate the fall from innocence of people who had assumed that finding wealth would erase their problems. Steinbeck had earlier written about such characters in his short story "Flight" and in *Tortilla Flat* (the *paisanos*—now Chicanos—of Monterey), as he would later write about a more racially mixed group in *Cannery Row* (Mack and his friends). He wrote, ironically, that these characters' good points—"kindness and generosity, openness, honesty, understanding and feeling"—were the traits most likely to lead to failure in the dog-eat-dog capitalistic system.

Steinbeck's life had been one of lower middle-class values as he learned the craft of writing. Born in 1902 in Monterey County, California, he grew up with Mexican American friends, and became fascinated by their lack of concern for more prestigious WASP values. He felt pulled between the two cultures. As a college student, he studied at Stanford University, majoring in marine biology, a science that attracted him by its beauty and systemic order. In 1925 he dropped out of school to work his way to New York City through the Panama Canal. There he worked as a journalist and practiced the art of writing, publishing a fictionalized life of Sir Henry Morgan (*Cup of Gold*) in 1929.

Returning to California, for two winters Steinbeck lived alone in the High Sierra mountains, writing and developing a philosophy that showed his respect for the symmetry and sensibility of the natural world. His personal pantheism replaced any other organized religion (in *Cannery Row*, his version of the Lord's Prayer begins "Our Father who art in nature"). He then worked in a trout hatchery and on fruit ranches (laboring with Mexican Americans in the orchards), and as a surveyor, an apprentice painter, and a chemist. In 1932 he published *Pastures of Heaven*, a collection of short stories about the working-class people who lived in the secluded valley of that name. In 1935, after he had sold the screen rights to *Tortilla Flat*, his fiction about the *paisanos* of Monterey, he took a trip to Mexico for several months.

As a native Californian, Steinbeck was aware of how much Mexico meant to the American culture that surrounded him, and he was curious about—and interested in—the country. It was becoming clear to him that any system of morality—one of the things for which he had searched during his years working outside the privileged occupations in the States—could sometimes be more easily found among the poor than among the financially successful. If Steinbeck was cynical, his cynicism at least had its roots in his real-life experiences. One result of that Mexican experience was *Of Mice and Men*, his 1937 novella that became a successful play, where he again probed the tragedy inherent in lives crippled by the brutality of poverty and ignorance. In Lennie's case, his retarded mind combined with his powerful physique led inexorably to predictable tragedies.

Between the often frightening reactions to *The Grapes of Wrath* and his earlier fiction, and Steinbeck's work on *The Pearl* in 1944, came other experiences that helped to confirm his feelings about the values of the poor who knew little except how to be genuine, truthful, and usually moral. He served as a journalist during World War II, living in danger on the Italian front. In contrast to that bleak, chaotic time, he had one of his most idyllic periods when, in the spring of 1940, he sailed with Ed Ricketts, his friend and partner in a small biological laboratory, from Monterey up the west shore of the Gulf of California to Angeles Bay and then across to Puerto San Carlos east and south to Agiabampo Estuary. During the six weeks of their travels in Baja, collecting marine and terrestrial organisms and animals, they lived among the Mexican people, whom they liked because of their tough yet humane values. So important was this journey to Steinbeck at this time in his life, rocked by the unexpected criticism of his work and slanderous innuendos, that, with Ricketts, he wrote *Sea of Cortez: A Leisurely Journal of Travel and Research*.

What he had thought to be the peace of California life, with its live-and-let-live attitude toward people of color, came to an abrupt halt in 1942 and 1943, when Los Angeles was racked by race riots. In the east-side barrios, Mexican and Mexican American adolescents and young men had formed *pachucos*, or gangs, and as uniforms wore wide-brimmed hats and long-tailed coats, complete with ankle-length watch chains. Dressed in these zoot suits, the Mexican men were targets for racial discrimination. The trial of twenty-four *pachucos* in the summer of 1942 for the murder of Jose Diaz near "The Sleepy Lagoon" swimming hole led to many convictions, and the men had served two years of their sentences before the second-degree murder convictions were overturned for lack of evidence. Even more visible were the ten days of the so-called Zoot Suit Race Riots in June of 1943, when U.S. servicemen from the Navy training facility in the barrio attacked the zoot-suited Mexicans. Abetted by police, the servicemen went free while the Mexicans were arrested. Like the unreasonable persecution of the Okies, this turn against people of Mexican background puzzled and angered Steinbeck.

During the early 1940s Steinbeck also wrote screenplays for four films, among them the documentary *The Forgotten Village*, about the conflicts between modern medicine and superstitious folk cures in a Mexican town. During the filming of that project, he returned to Mexico twice, and when he took his wife, Gwyn, for a third visit, friends there suggested that he write a screenplay for a film to be produced and filmed in Mexico, a film that might create a true picture of Mexican life because it could bypass the Hollywood studios. Emilio Fernandez, Mexico's best-known *auteur*, and Gebrial Figuora, his cinematographer, wanted to make the film with Steinbeck.

The Pearl, then, grew out of this invitation to write a text suitable for filming, and Steinbeck's strategies in it are often filmic: his use of only a few characters, action pared to key scenes that involve intensely emotional interchanges, and ways for readers/viewers to visualize that emotion. He also used a cinematic point of view, with some sections presented in close-up and others at medium or distant range. Like an objectively presented documentary text, *The Pearl* focused on showing the reader/viewer what life for Kino and Juana was like. Some of the elements of the story are drawn from *The Forgotten Village* (i.e., the rapacious physician), but the source of the narrative is much more clearly the tale of the young Mexican boy who finds a pearl of great value, a legend that Steinbeck narrated in *Sea of Cortez*. For the next several years, through his World War II experiences and his own unhappy personal life, Steinbeck searched for a story suitable for a Mexican-made and directed film. Dissatisfied as he had become with American materialism and the pressure to be loyal to a system that oppressed the poor, Steinbeck focused on the chance to write something truthful. He also hoped his screenplay would promote understanding among races.

As he thought about the pearl story, however, the legend seemed much too simple. In the *Sea of Cortez* narrative, the boy finding the pearl was intent on using it for money to buy drink, sex, and clothes. The tragedy in this version of the tale was that the pearl dealers in La Paz (the ironically named Village of Peace) would not give him a reasonable price for the pearl, and after realizing that he was the victim of their collusion, he buried the jewel. Owning such valuable property, he became the target for attack, and that night he was beaten. The next night, when he stayed with a friend, both boys were beaten; later, when he traveled away from the village, he was again tracked and beaten. So he returned to La Paz, dug up the pearl, cursed it, and threw it into the sea. In Steinbeck's words, "He was a free man again with his soul in danger and his food and shelter insecure. And he laughed a great deal about it." While a reader might question what was comic about an endangered soul and insecure living, one of Steinbeck's points was that, as a single man, his protagonist could take chances with life. His existence was not threatened by his giving up the fortune.

What was important about the legend as Steinbeck recalled it is that the boy had the sense to get rid of the object that was going to cost him his life. The original pearl story, then, is a parable of materialism, an example of the dangers of prosperity in a culture that thinks nothing of killing for money. But the pearl story as Steinbeck wrote it several years later is different, and it shows how complex his own state of mind was at this time of conjunction of war experience, Hollywood film experience, material success from *The Grapes of Wrath* and other ventures, with all the good things tempered radically by the deaths he had observed in the theater of war, as well as by the death of his marriage. The year 1944 was a time of personal change for John Steinbeck, and he was apprehensive about that change.

His personal situation influenced his creation of *The Pearl*. When Steinbeck wrote his version of the story, he made the young man into the older Kino, a responsible married man with a wife and child to provide for. Kino is probably named for Eusebius Kino, the Jesuit missionary and explorer in the Gulf region (it was he who proved that lower California was a peninsula—a *baja*—rather than an island). In *Sea of Cortez*, Steinbeck had shown his knowledge of many of the explorers and missionaries, both Mexican and American, involved with the settlement of the Baja. That journal too has a spiritual overlay, as Steinbeck used it to explore several sets of principles for leading a good life.

Juana, the name he chose for Kino's wife, means "woman," and as such she becomes the answerer, the solace for her husband's disappointed idealism. As in his earlier fiction, particularly in the characters of Ma and Pa Joad in

The Grapes of Wrath, Steinbeck drew male and female as complementary characters, with the woman having wisdom, common sense, and authority to balance the man's more wistful and sometimes unrealistic hopes. With tempered sympathy, Steinbeck acknowledges that Kino is obsessed with hanging on to the pearl, and that in equating it with his pride, he fails to see that his more useful role toward his family would be protecting them. When he confesses that the pearl has become his soul. Kino admits that he will endanger his family rather than relinquish his prize, and his abuse of Juana when she tries to get rid of the pearl illustrates his growing fanaticism. In that unexpected violence, Steinbeck shows how far from any Jungian individuation Kino's wealth has taken him—he is a monster of a male ego, not a caring and supportive husband. But behind Kino's obviously rash behavior stands the tranquil wife, who watches over him while he sleeps and starts the fire each morning. Though all-knowing and all caring, Juana in her role as submissive wife does not have enough power to make Kino listen to her warnings.

Juana is also the mother of Kino's most prized possession, his son, Coyotito. Kino says that his wish in finding the pearl and recognizing its value is that Coyotito be educated, that he become a savior figure to lead his village out of the abject poverty in which it exists. For most of the novella, Kino is so filled with this urgent hope that he does not hear Juana's counsel; her role becomes significant only near the end of the tragic tale, when the formative events have already occurred. Rather, Kino is led by an internal song he calls "The Song of the Family," a melody that haunts him with its sound; "this is safety, this is warmth, this is the *Whole*." In some respects, *The Pearl* is a parable of a personal journey toward that indivisible unity, or "wholeness," described by Carl Jung. Kino's dilemma over the pearl may also be read as a metaphor for his struggle to claim his unconscious self and integrate the "shadow" side, the femaleness within his male identity. He must come to see life, at least in part, as Juana does.

Narratively, Steinbeck complicates the parable of the pearl of great price when he adds the vulnerability of the baby, first introducing the child's helplessness in the scorpion scene. No matter how attentive his parents are, no matter that both are within arm's reach of the child, they cannot prevent the insect's biting him. Once bitten, the child becomes the object of attention, an icon to test people's values. The villagers know his worth to Kino and Juana; they understand Juana's desire that he receive formal medical treatment, and they follow the young family to the house of the doctor. But when the white man refuses to treat the child, they also understand that money is his only god, and Kino obviously is poor. Later, when the doctor reverses his position and comes to Kino's hut (only to poison the child and then give him an antidote—both visits serving as the means for him to look for the pearl's possible hiding place), the community also understands that duplicity. During the night, the physician sends someone to steal the jewel. He has put the family's real jewel, their son, at risk in the process of enabling himself to profit from Kino's simple luck.

Extending the plot to include a child, then, creates a kind of vulnerability that putting either Kino or Juana in danger would not have conveyed. The perversion of sheer innocence, and its ravishment, sets in motion a dynamic like that of medieval morality plays. Steinbeck, well read in medieval texts, created his own version of the fourteenth-century alliterative poem *Pearl*, an elegy by the anonymous poet for the death of his daughter before she was two years old. In this 1212-line poem, the sorrowful poet persona sees a vision of his child as the young woman she would have become. As a result of the dream or mystical experience, he plunges into a river, attempting to join his child in her blessed, heavenly state. His journey, a plunge into the dark night of the soul, leads to his awakening, and to his eventual acceptance of the child's loss. The poem closes with the poet's renunciation of his earthly pain: "Upon this hill this destiny I grasped, / Prostrate in sorrow for my pearl. / And afterward to God I gave it up." As the poet moves past his understandable grief for the loss of his child, he comes to realize the limits of human will and the confines of human consciousness. He places his trust in God.

Steinbeck transfers the resonance of the medieval legend to his own *Pearl* and forces the reader to see that Kino's journey to safeguard the pearl becomes an allegory of spiritual struggle. In the course of protecting the precious jewel, Kino kills a man who is nameless, formless, a kind of evil in himself—and he does so without remorse. As he takes more and more evil into his own behavior, finally killing three more men as he rationalizes that he must perform these acts to guard the pearl that will improve the lot of his family, Kino endangers his own morality. The explorations of his namesake in the Baja wilderness are tame compared with Kino's exploration of the levels of human sin. In the shifting value of the pearl—from great material worth into an objectification of sheer evil—Steinbeck leads the reader to see that its eventual loss will be a necessity.

Again, by focusing on the family dynamic, Steinbeck adds both life and complexity to his narrative. Kino is not an individual Everyman; he is husband and father as well as man. In fact, being parents complicates all decision making for both Kino and Juana: Kino justifies his wanting the money from the pearl to better his son's life; his is no selfish desire. Relinquishing the jewel consequently becomes almost impossible, for to give up the money the pearl will bring means relegating Coyotito to the kind of life he and his family have always known. But in a cyclic way, with so much hope invested in Coyotito, his vulnerability frightens both his parents. Juana insists that the doctor see him; Kino, at the farthest edge of his imagining—with the idea that his son could receive an education—begins to understand personal fear. His premonition of wrongdoing, that he has taken on something much larger than he can control, starts with that hopeful idea.

Kino's older brother, Juan Tomás, is another important addition to Steinbeck's reworking of the original legend. The reactions of Juan Tomás support Kino's almost inarticulate recognition of what is happening to him, giving the reader a way to verify that Kino's understanding is accurate. Because Steinbeck's setting for *The Pearl* is almost dreamlike, and certainly unspecific as to geographic location, to provide this confirming voice is necessary: This is a community, a set of people, a family; and yet for all the strength of their unity, they cannot stave off the evil that haunts Kino once he possesses the pearl. Juan Tomás as the older brother has a wider understanding: He knows that Kino has been cheated, but he also knows that they have all been cheated, through history. His is the voice of reason, the voice of continuity, and the voice of caution. Early in the novella he warns Kino that he has no model for what he is attempting—and he concludes that such ambition must be wrong, for no one else has attempted such an act.

Despite this warning, however, Juan Tomás is loyal to Kino; and Steinbeck is careful to set the inner circle of family and friends against the broader, suspect community. People in the inner circle want Kino to succeed, even though their imaginations are stunned with the thought of his undertaking. They serve as a Greek chorus to echo, and reify, Kino's thoughts. They literally follow him to see what he is going to do next, and their presence (and the muffled echo of their words as they explain to those farther away what is happening) serves as validation. In form, then, as well as in the undercurrent of doom that pervades *The Pearl*, Steinbeck creates the effects of the Greek tragedies he admired.

Linguistically, however, he abjured the stately and restrained language of Euripides and Sophocles. Yet in shaping voices for his Mexican speakers, he created a dignified speech that resonates with pain. Steinbeck had a difficult task in capturing a non-English-speaking culture in his own language, yet the chief movement in the narrative occurs in the dialogue, in the voiced interchanges among the Mexican characters. Kino must ask to see the doctor. When he is refused, and his paltry eight seed pearls are handed back through the fence to accompany the lie that the doctor is out, he gives up any attempt to speak and relies on force as he bashes his hand against the wrought-iron fence that closes against him. When he asks the pearl dealer for more money, his hesitant speech again cripples him—but Steinbeck makes it clear that no matter what his eloquence, the dealers' coalition would have kept the price low. In the moving scenes between Kino and Juana, few words are used, even though those scenes are decisive points in the narrative.

To replace verbal meaning, Steinbeck creates a technique suitable for a film script but unexpected in a written text: He uses music both to express mood and to replace dialogue. His "Song of the Family," a positive and encouraging sound, is set against the "Song of Evil" or the "Song of the Pearl." What happens in the struggles among the refrains anticipates the narrative conflicts. Steinbeck uses these musical motifs to suggest the complexity of Kino's decisions, as in his description of the "Song of the Family" underlying the "Song of Danger," when Kino is ready to take on the three trackers after he has hidden Juana and Coyotito in the cave. His slow descent into the morass of evil, naked so that his white clothing does not give him away, is surely a metaphor for the person going to meet the test of his life, for his soul, alone.

As Steinbeck forces the reader to listen for something other than language in *The Pearl*, he moves back toward an earlier culture of oral communication instead of written. (Jackson Benson notes that Steinbeck was reading folktales in Spanish as he began writing *The Pearl*, evidently looking for a tonal base that would allow him the resonance of that language without leaving the English his readers expected.) His use of the parable form was another means of insisting that Kino's story was archetypal, common to all human interaction. Steinbeck often used literary forms in ironic ways: Here, the parable that instructs non-believers in what they must do to enter the kingdom of heaven takes on a kind of sly cynicism as it becomes a vehicle to picture a corrupt and murderous culture. The morality inscribed in

The Pearl is a reverse kind of instruction: Kino has done nothing wrong except fail to recognize evil when it appears (in the object of the beautiful pearl). He can live as pure a life as he knows, but nothing will bring sanity back into his existence except getting rid of the object of beauty. His community cannot help him; neither can he help himself, unaware and unsuspecting as he is. The irony of Steinbeck's pearl narrative is that no god appears to save Kino, his child, or his family. He must save himself—and he can do that only by reconciling the female with the male, only by listening to Juana.

His wife speaks wisely throughout the narrative when she tells him repeatedly that the pearl is evil and would destroy them, but it remains for Kino to learn to live with tragedy before he can hear her. (Steinbeck shows Juana's broad philosophical base when he remarks that she draws on a "combination of prayer and magic, her Hail Marys and her ancient intercession.") As the book ends, Kino's offering her the pearl so that she can throw it away is his apology for his obtuseness, his sinful error in failing to understand that greed can corrupt the soul. Her refusing the jewel so that he can empower himself by casting it into the sea is Juana's means of allowing Kino to reclaim some part of his badly damaged manhood. This interplay between husband and wife suggests that their marriage will survive the death of their child, but Steinbeck has also created such a poignant tenor of mourning that few readers expect either Kino or Juana to recover their earlier happiness.

The metaphoric qualities of *The Pearl* convey much of its meaning. For some readers, the bleak ending of the novella is despairing—and disspiriting. For others, responsive to Steinbeck's musical motifs and the obvious harmony in the resolve of Juana and Kino to get rid of the pearl, the ending is a relief, a release, as the couple attempt to go back to their earlier life. Steinbeck suggests that Kino has learned to accept defeat, and his attitude toward the tragic death of Coyotito is the appropriate one of ineradicable grief for the loss of a human being, rather than the anger at his own loss of his male heir.

Steinbeck has also made it clear that losing the pearl is inevitable: Power accrues to those who already have it. Neither Kino nor his family nor his community have any chance of hanging on to the prize fortune has accidentally given them. Understanding that they are fortunate to have their lives, given the rapacity of most human beings (even, or particularly, the doctor), Kino and Juana are reconciled to live their poor lives with gratefulness. It is less a happy ending than it is a stoically resolved one.

The narrative that Steinbeck thought he would write was subtly changed in his telling. His recent biographer Jackson Benson sees *The Pearl* as a reflection of the synthesis taking place within Steinbeck. His ongoing scientific studies provided the ideas that "would form a bridge from his early work, poetic and visionary, to the so-called sociological works of the middle period, from *In Dubious Battle* to *The Pearl*." Benson calls attention to the discrepancy in nomenclature: These works are literature, not sociology. But in them Steinbeck's concern for the real lives of characters that might exist dominates his portraiture. His personal sympathy for the down-and-out of society—whether in the States or in Mexico—led him to draw their circumstances vividly. Steinbeck's fiction provides convincing details, so that the reader believes in the characters' dilemmas.

In the weeks he spent in 1944 getting ready to write *The*

Pearl, Steinbeck found "the little book" more difficult to complete than he had expected. To a friend, he wrote that he had visited the "beautiful" ruins of Mitla and Monte Alban near Oaxaca, as well as San Miguel Allende, commenting on the strangeness of his impressions and his sense that he was experiencing a personal rebirth. After he had finished *Cannery Row*, and Gwyn had given birth to their son, Thom, he was able to begin work on *The Pearl* in earnest. Once the family was settled down and living together, Steinbeck felt that his life was once more whole, and Gwyn then helped write the theme music from what he described as "ancient Indian music long preceding the Conquest."

Working on *The Pearl* was an unusual process, one that absorbed much of Steinbeck's energies. He commented about its being so experimental that he feared it would fail; in a letter to friends, he called the story "folklore" and noted that he had tried "to give it that set-aside, raised-up feeling that all folk stories have." Once *The Pearl* was finished, in late January of 1945, he wrote with his usual modesty, "It's a brutal story but with flashes of beauty I think."

The process of filming the work dragged on through the summer of 1945, but in 1947 and 1948, it became the first Mexican-made film to be commercially distributed in the States. *The Pearl* was published in 1947 to coincide with the film's release, though it had earlier appeared as *The Pearl of the World* in the December 1945 issue of *The Woman's Home Companion*. The reaction to Steinbeck's nativity story—with Kino, Juana, and Coyotito as his Holy Family—was unimpressive. Although some critics today consider it one of his best postwar accomplishments, it was often dismissed when it was reviewed at all as too slight an effort to warrant serious criticism. Louis Owens speaks to that body of what he calls "contradictory criticism" of *The Pearl*, ranging from calling the novella "defective" to a "triumph." In contrast, readers of the 1990s came to appreciate the work's broadly based sympathies, its rare understanding of otherness, its insistence on a man's achieving his own psychological health, and its eloquent lyricism that remains in the reader's eye and ear as if it were almost a visualization of Kino and Juana's travail.

Suggestions for Further Reading

Benson, Jackson J., ed. *The Short Novels of John Steinbeck*.
Durham, N.C.: Duke University Press, 1990.
—. *The True Adventures of John Steinbeck, Writer*. New
York: Viking, 1984.
Britch, Carroll, and Cliff Lewis. "Shadow of The Indian in
the Fiction of John Steinbeck." In *Rediscovering Stein-
beck: Revisionist Views of His Art, Politics, and Intellect*,
ed. Cliff Lewis and Carroll Britch. Lewiston, Va.: Edwin
Mellen, 1989, pp. 125–154.
Davis, Robert Murray, ed. *Steinbeck: A Collection of Criti-
cal Essays*. Englewood Cliffs, N.J.: Prentice-Hall, 1972.
DeMott, Robert J. *Steinbeck's Reading*. New York: Gar-
land, 1984.
Fontenrose, Joseph. "*Sea of Cortez*." In Davis, *Steinbeck:
A Collection of Critical Essays*, pp. 122–134.
Garza, Rodolfo O. de la, et. al., eds. *The Mexican American
Experience: An Interdisciplinary Anthology*. Austin: Uni-
versity of Texas Press, 1985.
Gladstein, Mimi Reisel. *The Indestructible Woman in
Faulkner, Hemingway, and Steinbeck*. Ann Arbor: Uni-
versity of Michigan Research Press, 1986.
Hayashi, Tetsumaro, ed. *John Steinbeck, The Years of*

Greatness, 1936–1939. Tuscaloosa: University of Alabama Press, 1993.

Hughes, R. S. *John Steinbeck: A Study of the Short Fiction*. Boston: Twayne, 1989.

Jung, Carl G. *The Archetypes and the Collective Unconscious*, ed. Sir Herbert Read, et. al. 2nd ed., vol. 9 [1] of *The Collected Works of C. G. Jung* (New York: Bollingen Foundation, Inc., 1975).

Kiernan, Thomas. *The Intricate Music: A Biography of John Steinbeck*. Boston: Little, Brown, 1979.

Lisca, Peter. *The Wide World of John Steinbeck*. New Brunswick, N.J.: Rutgers University Press, 1958; rpt. New York: Gordian Press, 1981.

Millichap, Joseph R. *Steinbeck and Film*. New York: Frederick Ungar, 1983.

Morris, Harry. *"The Pearl*: Realism and Allegory." In Davis, *Steinbeck: A Collection of Critical Essays*, pp. 149–162.

Owens, Louis. *John Steinbeck's Re-Vision of America*, Athens: University of Georgia Press, 1985.

Simmonds, Roy S. "Steinbeck's *The Pearl*: Legend, Film, Novel." In Benson, *The Short Novels of John Steinbeck*, pp. 173–184.

—. "Steinbeck's *The Pearl*: A Preliminary Textual Study." *Steinbeck Quarterly* 22 (Winter–Spring, 1989), pp. 16–34.

St. Pierre, Brian. *John Steinbeck, the California Years*. San Francisco, Calif.: Chronicle Books, 1983.

Steinbeck, Elaine, and Robert Wallsten, eds. *Steinbeck: A Life in Letters*, New York: Viking, 1975.

Steinbeck, John. *Cannery Row*. New York: Viking, 1945.

—. *The Grapes of Wrath*. New York: Viking, 1939.

—. "My Short Novels." In Benson, *The Short Novels of John Steinbeck*, pp. 15–17.

—. *The Pearl*. New York: Viking, 1947.

—. with Edward F. Ricketts. *Sea of Cortez: A Leisurely Journal of Travel and Research*. New York: Viking, 1941.

—. with Edward F. Ricketts. *The Log from The Sea of Cortez*, ed. Richard Astro. Minneapolis: University of Minnesota Press, 1973.

Timmerman, John H. "The Shadow and the Pearl: Jungian Patterns in *The Pearl*." In Benson, *The Short Novels of John Steinbeck*, pp. 143–161.

The Pearl

"In the town they tell the story of the great pearl—how it was found and how it was lost again. They tell of Kino, the fisherman, and of his wife, Juana, and of the baby, Coyotito. And because the story has been told so often, it has taken root in every man's mind. And, as with all retold tales that are in people's hearts, there are only good and bad things and black and white things and good and evil things and no in-between anywhere.

"If this story is a parable, perhaps everyone takes his own meaning from it and reads his own life into it. In any case, they say in the town that . . ."

1

Kino awakened in the near dark. The stars still shone and the day had drawn only a pale wash of light in the lower sky to the east. The roosters had been crowing for some time, and the early pigs were already beginning their ceaseless turning of twigs and bits of wood to see whether anything to eat had been overlooked. Outside the brush house in the tuna clump, a covey of little birds chittered and flurried with their wings.

Kino's eyes opened, and he looked first at the lightening square which was the door and then he looked at the hanging box where Coyotito slept. And last he turned his head to Juana, his wife, who lay beside him on the mat, her blue head shawl over her nose and over her breasts and around the small of her back. Juana's eyes were open too. Kino could never remember seeing them closed when he awakened. Her dark eyes made little reflected stars. She was looking at him as she was always looking at him when he awakened.

Kino heard the little splash of morning waves on the beach. It was very good—Kino closed his eyes again to listen to his music. Perhaps he alone did this and perhaps all of his people did it. His people had once been great makers of songs so that everything they saw or thought or did or heard became a song. That was very long ago. The songs remained; Kino knew them, but no new songs were added. That does not mean that there were no personal songs. In Kino's head there was a song now, clear and soft, and if he had been able to speak of it, he would have called it the Song of the Family.

His blanket was over his nose to protect him from the dank air. His eyes flicked to a rustle beside him. It was Juana arising, almost soundlessly. On her hard bare feet she went to the hanging box where Coyotito slept, and she leaned over and said a little reassuring word. Coyotito looked up for a moment and closed his eyes and slept again.

Juana went to the fire pit and uncovered a coal and fanned it alive while she broke little pieces of brush over it.

Now Kino got up and wrapped his blanket about his head and nose and shoulders. He slipped his feet into his sandals and went outside to watch the dawn.

Outside the door he squatted down and gathered the blanket ends about his knees. He saw the specks of Gulf clouds flame high in the air. And a goat came near and sniffed at him and stared with its cold yellow eyes. Behind him Juana's fire leaped into flame and threw spears of light through the chinks of the brushhouse wall and threw a wavering square of light out the door. A late moth blustered in to find the fire. The Song of the Family came now from behind Kino. And the rhythm of the family song was the grinding stone where Juana worked the corn for the morning cakes.

The dawn came quickly now, a wash, a glow, a lightness, and then an explosion of fire as the sun arose out of the Gulf. Kino looked down to cover his eyes from the glare. He could hear the pat of the corncakes in the house and the rich smell of them on the cooking plate. The ants were busy on the ground, big black ones with shiny bodies, and little dusty quick ants. Kino watched with the detachment of God while a dusty ant frantically tried to escape the sand trap an ant lion had dug for him. A thin, timid dog came close and, at a soft word from Kino, curled up, arranged its tail neatly over its feet, and laid its chin delicately on the pile. It was a black dog with yellow-gold spots where its eyebrows should have been. It was a morning like other mornings and yet perfect among mornings.

Kino heard the creak of the rope when Juana took Coyotito out of his hanging box and cleaned him and hammocked him in her shawl in a loop that placed him close to her breast. Kino could see these things without looking at them. Juana sang softly an ancient song that had only three notes and yet endless variety of interval. And this was part of the family song too. It was all part. Sometimes it rose to an aching chord that caught the throat, saying this is safety, this is warmth, this is the *Whole*.

Across the brush fence were other brush houses, and the smoke came from them too, and the sound of breakfast, but those were other songs, their pigs were other pigs, their wives were not Juana. Kino was young and strong and his black hair hung over his brown forehead. His eyes were warm and fierce and bright and his mustache was thin and coarse. He lowered his blanket from his nose now, for the dark poisonous air was gone and the yellow sunlight fell on the house. Near the brush fence two roosters bowed and feinted at each other with squared wings and neck feathers ruffed out. It would be a clumsy fight. They were not game chickens. Kino watched them for a moment, and then his eyes went up to a flight of wild doves twinkling inland to the hills. The world was awake now, and Kino arose and went into his brush house.

As he came through the door Juana stood up from the glowing fire pit. She put Coyotito back in his hanging box and then she combed her black hair and braided it in two braids and tied the ends with thin green ribbon. Kino squatted by the fire pit and rolled a hot corncake and dipped it in sauce and ate it. And he drank a little pulque and that was breakfast. That was the only breakfast he had ever known outside of feast days and one incredible fiesta on cookies that had nearly killed him. When Kino had finished, Juana came back to the fire and ate her breakfast. They had spoken once, but there is not need for speech if it is only a habit anyway. Kino sighed with satisfaction—and that was conversation.

The sun was warming the brush house, breaking through its crevices in long streaks. And one of the streaks fell on the hanging box where Coyotito lay, and on the ropes that held it.

It was a tiny movement that drew their eyes to the hanging box. Kino and Juana froze in their positions. Down the rope that hung the baby's box from the roof support a scorpion moved slowly. His stinging tail was straight out behind him, but he could whip it up in a flash of time.

Kino's breath whistled in his nostrils and he opened his mouth to stop it. And then the startled look was gone from him and the rigidity from his body. In his mind a new song had come, the Song of Evil, the music of the enemy, of any foe of the family, a savage, secret, dangerous melody, and underneath, the Song of the Family cried plaintively.

The scorpion moved delicately down the rope toward the box. Under her breath Juana repeated an ancient magic to guard against such evil, and on top of that she muttered

a Hail Mary between clenched teeth. But Kino was in
motion. His body glided quietly across the room, noiselessly
and smoothly. His hands were in front of him, palms down,
and his eyes were on the scorpion. Beneath it in the hanging
box Coyotito laughed and reached up his hand toward it. It
sensed danger when Kino was almost within reach of it. It
stopped, and its tail rose up over its back in little jerks and
the curved thorn on the tail's end glistened.

Kino stood perfectly still. He could hear Juana whispering the old magic again, and he could hear the evil music
of the enemy. He could not move until the scorpion moved,
and it felt for the source of the death that was coming to it.
Kino's hand went forward very slowly, very smoothly. The
thorned tail jerked upright. And at that moment the laugh-
ing Coyotito shook the rope and the scorpion fell.

Kino's hand leaped to catch it, but it fell past his fingers,
fell on the baby's shoulder, landed and struck. Then, snarl-
ing, Kino had it, had it in his fingers, rubbing it to a paste
in his hands. He threw it down and beat it into the earth
floor with his fist, and Coyotito screamed with pain in his
box. But Kino beat and stamped the enemy until it was only
a fragment and a moist place in the dirt. His teeth were
bared and fury flared in his eyes and the Song of the Enemy
roared in his ears.

But Juana had the baby in her arms now. She found the
puncture with redness starting from it already. She put her
lips down over the puncture and sucked hard and spat and
sucked again while Coyotito screamed.

Kino hovered; he was helpless, he was in the way.

The screams of the baby brought the neighbors. Out of
their brush houses they poured—Kino's brother Juan
Tomás and his fat wife Apolonia and their four children

crowded in the door and blocked the entrance, while behind them others tried to look in, and one small boy crawled among legs to have a look. And those in front passed the word back to those behind—"Scorpion. The baby has been stung."

Juana stopped sucking the puncture for a moment. The little hole was slightly enlarged and its edges whitened from the sucking, but the red swelling extended farther around it in a hard lymphatic mound. And all of these people knew about the scorpion. An adult might be very ill from the sting, but a baby could easily die from the poison. First, they knew, would come swelling and fever and tightened throat, and then cramps in the stomach, and then Coyotito might die if enough of the poison had gone in. But the stinging pain of the bite was going away. Coyotito's screams turned to moans.

Kino had wondered often at the iron in his patient, fragile wife. She, who was obedient and respectful and cheerful and patient, she could arch her back in child pain with hardly a cry. She could stand fatigue and hunger almost better than Kino himself. In the canoe she was like a strong man. And now she did a most surprising thing.

"The doctor," she said. "Go to get the doctor."

The word was passed out among the neighbors where they stood close packed in the little yard behind the brush fence. And they repeated among themselves, "Juana wants the doctor." A wonderful thing, a memorable thing, to want the doctor. To get him would be a remarkable thing. The doctor never came to the cluster of brush houses. Why should he, when he had more than he could do to take care of the rich people who lived in the stone and plaster houses of the town.

"He would not come," the people in the yard said.

"He would not come," the people in the door said, and the thought got into Kino.

"The doctor would not come," Kino said to Juana.

She looked up at him, her eyes as cold as the eyes of a lioness. This was Juana's first baby—this was nearly everything there was in Juana's world. And Kino saw her determination and the music of the family sounded in his head with a steely tone.

"Then we will go to him," Juana said, and with one hand she arranged her dark blue shawl over her head and made of one end of it a sling to hold the moaning baby and made of the other end of it a shade over his eyes to protect him from the light. The people in the door pushed against those behind to let her through. Kino followed her. They went out of the gate to the rutted path and the neighbors followed them.

The thing had become a neighborhood affair. They made a quick soft-footed procession into the center of the town, first Juana and Kino, and behind them Juan Tomás and Apolonia, her big stomach jiggling with the strenuous pace, then all the neighbors with the children trotting on the flanks. And the yellow sun threw their black shadows ahead of them so that they walked on their own shadows.

They came to the place where the brush houses stopped and the city of stone and plaster began, the city of harsh outer walls and inner cool gardens where a little water played and the bougainvillaea crusted the walls with purple and brick-red and white. They heard from the secret gardens the singing of caged birds and heard the splash of cooling water on hot flagstones. The procession crossed the blinding plaza and passed in front of the church. It had grown now, and on the outskirts the hurrying newcomers

were being softly informed how the baby had been stung by a scorpion, how the father and mother were taking it to the doctor.

And the newcomers, particularly the beggars from the front of the church who were great experts in financial analysis, looked quickly at Juana's old blue skirt, saw the tears in her shawl, appraised the green ribbon on her braids, read the age of Kino's blanket and the thousand washings of his clothes, and set them down as poverty people and went along to see what kind of drama might develop. The four beggars in front of the church knew everything in the town. They were students of the expressions of young women as they went in to confession, and they saw them as they came out and read the nature of the sin. They knew every little scandal and some very big crimes. They slept at their posts in the shadow of the church so that no one crept in for consolation without their knowledge. And they knew the doctor. They knew his ignorance, his cruelty, his avarice, his appetites, his sins. They knew his clumsy abortions and the little brown pennies he gave sparingly for alms. They had seen his corpses go into the church. And, since early Mass was over and business was slow, they followed the procession, these endless searchers after perfect knowledge of their fellow men, to see what the fat lazy doctor would do about an indigent baby with a scorpion bite.

The scurrying procession came at last to the big gate in the wall of the doctor's house. They could hear the splashing water and the singing of caged birds and the sweep of the long brooms on the flagstones. And they could smell the frying of good bacon from the doctor's house.

Kino hesitated a moment. This doctor was not of his people. This doctor was of a race which for nearly four hundred years had beaten and starved and robbed and despised Kino's race, and frightened it too, so that the indigene came humbly to the door. And as always when he came near to one of this race, Kino felt weak and afraid and angry at the same time. Rage and terror went together. He could kill the doctor more easily than he could talk to him, for all of the doctor's race spoke to all of Kino's race as though they were simple animals. And as Kino raised his right hand to the iron ring knocker in the gate, rage swelled in him, and the pounding music of the enemy beat in his ears, and his lips drew tight against his teeth—but with his left hand he reached to take off his hat. The iron ring pounded against the gate. Kino took off his hat and stood waiting. Coyotito moaned a little in Juana's arms, and she spoke softly to him. The procession crowded close the better to see and hear.

After a moment the big gate opened a few inches. Kino could see the green coolness of the garden and little splashing fountain through the opening. The man who looked out at him was one of his own race. Kino spoke to him in the old language. "The little one—the first born—has been poisoned by the scorpion," Kino said. "He requires the skill of the healer."

The gate closed a little, and the servant refused to speak in the old language. "A little moment," he said. "I go to inform myself," and he closed the gate and slid the bolt home. The glaring sun threw the bunched shadows of the people blackly on the white wall.

In his chamber the doctor sat up in his high bed. He had on his dressing gown of red watered silk that had come from Paris, a little tight over the chest now if it was buttoned. On his lap was a silver tray with a silver chocolate pot and a tiny cup of eggshell china, so delicate that it looked silly when he lifted it with his big hand, lifted it with the tips of thumb and forefinger and spread the other three fingers wide to get them out of the way. His eyes rested in puffy little hammocks of flesh and his mouth drooped with discontent. He was growing very stout, and his voice was hoarse with the fat that pressed on his throat. Beside him on a table was a small Oriental gong and a bowl of cigarettes. The furnishings of the room were heavy and dark and gloomy. The pictures were religious, even the large tinted photograph of his dead wife, who, if Masses willed and paid for out of her own estate could do it, was in Heaven. The doctor had once for a short time been a part of the great world and his whole subsequent life was memory and longing for France. "That," he said, "was civilized living"—by which he meant that, on a small income he had been able to keep a mistress and eat in restaurants. He poured his second cup of chocolate and crumbled a sweet biscuit in his fingers. The servant from the gate came to the open door and stood waiting to be noticed.

"Yes?" the doctor asked.

"It is a little Indian with a baby. He says a scorpion stung it."

The doctor put his cup down gently before he let his anger rise.

"Have I nothing better to do than cure insect bites for 'little Indians'? I am a doctor, not a veterinary."

"Yes, Patron," said the servant.

"Has he any money?" the doctor demanded. "No, they never have any money. I, I alone in the world am supposed to work for nothing—and I am tired of it. See if he has any money!"

At the gate the servant opened the door a trifle and looked out at the waiting people. And this time he spoke in the old language.

"Have you money to pay for the treatment?"

Now Kino reached into a secret place somewhere under his blanket. He brought out a paper folded many times. Crease by crease he unfolded it, until at last there came to view eight small misshapen seed pearls, as ugly and gray as little ulcers, flattened and almost valueless. The servant took the paper and closed the gate again, but this time he was not gone long. He opened the gate just wide enough to pass the paper back.

"The doctor has gone out," he said. "He was called to a serious case." And he shut the gate quickly out of shame.

And now a wave of shame went over the whole procession. They melted away. The beggars went back to the church steps, the stragglers moved off, and the neighbors departed so that the public shaming of Kino would not be in their eyes.

For a long time Kino stood in front of the gate with Juana beside him. Slowly he put his suppliant hat on his head. Then, without warning, he struck the gate a crushing blow with his fist. He looked down in wonder at his split knuckles and at the blood that flowed down between his fingers.

2

The town lay on a broad estuary, its old yellow plastered buildings hugging the beach. And on the beach the white and blue canoes that came from Nayarit were drawn up, canoes preserved for generations by a hard shell-like water-proof plaster whose making was a secret of the fishing people. They were high and graceful canoes with curving bow and stern and a braced section midships where a mast could be stepped to carry a small lateen sail.

The beach was yellow sand, but at the water's edge a rubble of shell and algae took its place. Fiddler crabs bubbled and sputtered in their holes in the sand, and in the shallows little lobsters popped in and out of their tiny homes in the rubble and sand. The sea bottom was rich with crawling and swimming and growing things. The brown algae waved in the gentle currents and the green eel grass swayed and little sea horses clung to its stems. Spotted botete, the poison fish, lay on the bottom in the eel-grass beds, and the bright-colored swimming crabs scampered over them.

On the beach the hungry dogs and the hungry pigs of the town searched endlessly for any dead fish or sea bird that might have floated in on a rising tide.

Although the morning was young, the hazy mirage was

up. The uncertain air that magnified some things and blotted out others hung over the whole Gulf so that all sights were unreal and vision could not be trusted; so that sea and land had the sharp clarities and the vagueness of a dream. Thus it might be that the people of the Gulf trust things of the spirit and things of the imagination, but they do not trust their eyes to show them distance or clear outline or any optical exactness. Across the estuary from the town one section of mangroves stood clear and telescopically defined, while another mangrove clump was a hazy black-green blob. Part of the far shore disappeared into a shimmer that looked like water. There was no certainty in seeing, no proof that what you saw was there or was not there. And the people of the Gulf expected all places were that way, and it was not strange to them. A copper haze hung over the water, and the hot morning sun beat on it and made it vibrate blindingly.

The brush houses of the fishing people were back from the beach on the right-hand side of the town, and the canoes were drawn up in front of this area.

Kino and Juana came slowly down to the beach and to Kino's canoe, which was the one thing of value he owned in the world. It was very old. Kino's grandfather had brought it from Nayarit, and he had given it to Kino's father, and so it had come to Kino. It was at once property and source of food, for a man with a boat can guarantee a woman that she will eat something. It is the bulwark against starvation. And every year Kino refinished his canoe with the hard shell-like plaster by the secret method that had also come to him from his father. Now he came to the canoe and touched the bow tenderly as he always did. He laid his diving rock and his basket and the two ropes in the sand by the canoe. And he folded his blanket and laid it in the bow.

Juana laid Coyotito on the blanket, and she placed her shawl over him so that the hot sun could not shine on him. He was quiet now, but the swelling on his shoulder had continued up his neck and under his ear and his face was puffed and feverish. Juana went to the water and waded in. She gathered some brown seaweed and made a flat damp poultice of it, and this she applied to the baby's swollen shoulder, which was as good a remedy as any and probably better than the doctor could have done. But the remedy lacked his authority because it was simple and didn't cost anything. The stomach cramps had not come to Coyotito. Perhaps Juana had sucked out the poison in time, but she had not sucked out her worry over her first-born. She had not prayed directly for the recovery of the baby—she had prayed that they might find a pearl with which to hire the doctor to cure the baby, for the minds of people are as unsubstantial as the mirage of the Gulf.

Now Kino and Juana slid the canoe down the beach to the water, and when the bow floated, Juana climbed in, while Kino pushed the stern in and waded beside it until it floated lightly and trembled on the little breaking waves. Then in co-ordination Juana and Kino drove their double-bladed paddles into the sea, and the canoe creased the water and hissed with speed. The other pearlers were gone out long since. In a few moments Kino could see them clustered in the haze, riding over the oyster bed.

Light filtered down through the water to the bed where the frilly pearl oysters lay fastened to the rubbly bottom, a bottom strewn with shells of broken, opened oysters. This was the bed that had raised the King of Spain to be a great power in Europe in past years, had helped to pay for his wars, and had decorated the churches for his soul's sake. The gray oysters with ruffles like skirts on the shells, the barnacle-crusted oysters with little bits of weed clinging to the skirts and small crabs climbing over them. An accident could happen to these oysters, a grain of sand could lie in the folds of muscle and irritate the flesh until in self-protection the flesh coated the grain with a layer of smooth cement. But once started, the flesh continued to coat the foreign body until it fell free in some tidal flurry or until the oyster was destroyed. For centuries men had dived down and torn the oysters from the beds and ripped them open, looking for the coated grains of sand. Swarms of fish lived near the bed to live near the oysters thrown back by the searching men and to nibble at the shining inner shells. But the pearls were accidents, and the finding of one was luck, a little pat on the back by God or the gods or both.

Kino had two ropes, one tied to a heavy stone and one to a basket. He stripped off his shirt and trousers and laid his hat in the bottom of the canoe. The water was oily smooth. He took his rock in one hand and his basket in the other, and he slipped feet first over the side and the rock carried him to the bottom. The bubbles rose behind him until the water cleared and he could see. Above, the surface of the water was an undulating mirror of brightness, and he could see the bottoms of the canoes sticking through it.

Kino moved cautiously so that the water would not be obscured with mud or sand. He hooked his foot in the loop on his rock and his hands worked quickly, tearing the oysters loose, some singly, others in clusters. He laid them in his basket. In some places the oysters clung to one another so that they came free in lumps.

Now, Kino's people had sung of everything that happened or existed. They had made songs to the fishes, to the sea in anger and to the sea in calm, to the light and the dark and the sun and the moon, and the songs were all in Kino and in his people—every song that had ever been made, even the ones forgotten. And as he filled his basket the song was in Kino, and the beat of the song was his pounding heart as it ate the oxygen from his held breath, and the melody of the song was the gray-green water and the little scuttling animals and the clouds of fish that flitted by and were gone. But in the song there was a secret little inner song, hardly perceptible, but always there, sweet and secret and clinging, almost hiding in the counter-melody, and this was the Song of the Pearl That Might Be, for every shell thrown in the basket might contain a pearl. Chance was against it, but luck and the gods might be for it. And in the canoe above him Kino knew that Juana was making the magic of prayer, her face set rigid and her muscles hard to force the luck, to tear the luck out of the gods' hands, for she needed the luck for the swollen shoulder of Coyotito. And because the need was great and the desire was great, the little secret melody of the pearl that might be was stronger this morning. Whole phrases of it came clearly and softly into the Song of the Undersea.

Kino, in his pride and youth and strength, could remain down over two minutes without strain, so that he worked deliberately, selecting the largest shells. Because they were disturbed, the oyster shells were tightly closed. A little to his right a hummock of rubbly rock stuck up, covered with young oysters not ready to take. Kino moved next to the hummock, and then, beside it, under a little overhang, he saw a very large oyster lying by itself not covered with its clinging brothers. The shell was partly open, for the overhang protected this ancient oyster, and in the lip-like muscle Kino saw a ghostly gleam, and then the shell closed down. His heart beat out a heavy rhythm and the melody of the maybe pearl shrilled in his ears. Slowly he forced the oyster loose and held it tightly against his breast. He kicked his foot free from the rock loop, and his body rose to the surface and his black hair gleamed in the sunlight. He reached over the side of the canoe and laid the oyster in the bottom.

Then Juana steadied the boat while he climbed in. His eyes were shining with excitement, but in decency he pulled up his rock, and then he pulled up his basket of oysters and lifted them in. Juana sensed his excitement, and she pretended to look away. It is not good to want a thing too much. It sometimes drives the luck away. You must want it just enough, and you must be very tactful with God or the gods. But Juana stopped breathing. Very deliberately Kino opened his short strong knife. He looked speculatively at the basket. Perhaps it would be better to open *the* oyster last. He took a small oyster from the basket, cut the muscle, searched the folds of flesh, and threw it in the water. Then he seemed to see the great, oyster for the first time. He squatted in the bottom of the canoe, picked up the shell and examined it. The flutes were shining black to brown, and only a few small barnacles adhered to the shell. Now Kino was reluctant to open it. What he had seen, he knew, might be a reflection, a piece of flat shell accidentally drifted in or a complete illusion. In this Gulf of uncertain light there were more illusions than realities.

But Juana's eyes were on him and she could not wait. She put her hand on Coyotito's covered head. "Open it," she said softly.

Kino deftly slipped his knife into the edge of the shell. Through the knife he could feel the muscle tighten hard. He worked the blade lever-wise and the closing muscle parted and the shell fell apart. The lip-like flesh writhed up and then subsided. Kino lifted the flesh, and there it lay, the great pearl, perfect as the moon. It captured the light and refined it and gave it back in silver incandescence. It was as large as a sea-gull's egg. It was the greatest pearl in the world.

Juana caught her breath and moaned a little. And to Kino the secret melody of the maybe pearl broke clear and beautiful, rich and warm and lovely, glowing and gloating and triumphant. In the surface of the great pearl he could see dream forms. He picked the pearl from the dying flesh and held it in his palm, and he turned it over and saw that its curve was perfect. Juana came near to stare at it in his hand, and it was the hand he had smashed against the doctor's gate, and the torn flesh of the knuckles was turned grayish white by the sea water.

Instinctively Juana went to Coyotito where he lay on his father's blanket. She lifted the poultice of seaweed and looked at the shoulder. "Kino," she cried shrilly.

He looked past his pearl, and he saw that the swelling was going out of the baby's shoulder, the poison was receding from its body. Then Kino's fist closed over the pearl and his emotion broke over him. He put back his head and howled. His eyes rolled up and he screamed and his body was rigid. The men in the other canoes looked up, startled, and then they dug their paddles into the sea and raced toward Kino's canoe.

3

A town is a thing like a colonial animal. A town has a nervous system and a head and shoulders and feet. A town is a thing separate from all other towns, so that there are no two towns alike. And a town has a whole emotion. How news travels through a town is a mystery not easily to be solved. News seems to move faster than small boys can scramble and dart to tell it, faster than women can call it over the fences.

Before Kino and Juana and the other fishers had come to Kino's brush house, the nerves of the town were pulsing and vibrating with the news—Kino had found the Pearl of the World. Before panting little boys could strangle out the words, their mothers knew it. The news swept on past the brush houses, and it washed in a foaming wave into the town of stone and plaster. It came to the priest walking in his garden, and it put a thoughtful look in his eyes and a memory of certain repairs necessary to the church. He wondered what the pearl would be worth. And he wondered whether he had baptized Kino's baby, or married him for that matter. The news came to the shopkeepers, and they looked at men's clothes that had not sold so well.

The news came to the doctor where he sat with a woman whose illness was age, though neither she nor the doctor would admit it. And when it was made plain who Kino was, the doctor grew stern and judicious at the same time. "He is a client of mine," the doctor said. "I am treating his child for a scorpion sting." And the doctor's eyes rolled up a little in their fat hammocks and he thought of Paris. He remembered the room he had lived in there as a great and luxurious place, and he remembered the hard-faced woman who had lived with him as a beautiful and kind girl, although she had been none of these three. The doctor looked past his aged patient and saw himself sitting in a restaurant in Paris and a waiter was just opening a bottle of wine.

The news came early to the beggars in front of the church, and it made them giggle a little with pleasure, for they knew that there is no almsgiver in the world like a poor man who is suddenly lucky.

Kino had found the Pearl of the World. In the town, in little offices, sat the men who bought pearls from the fishers. They waited in their chairs until the pearls came in, and then they cackled and fought and shouted and threatened until they reached the lowest price the fisherman would stand. But there was a price below which they dared not go, for it had happened that a fisherman in despair had given his pearls to the church. And when the buying was over, these buyers sat alone and their fingers played restlessly with the pearls, and they wished they owned the pearls. For there were not many buyers really—there was only one, and he kept these agents in separate offices to give a semblance of competition. The news came to these men, and their eyes squinted and their fingertips burned a little, and each one thought how the patron could not live forever and someone had to take his place. And each one thought how with some capital he could get a new start.

All manner of people grew interested in Kino—people with things to sell and people with favors to ask. Kino had found the Pearl of the World. The essence of pearl mixed with essence of men and a curious dark residue was precipitated. Every man suddenly became related to Kino's pearl, and Kino's pearl went into the dreams, the speculations, the schemes, the plans, the futures, the wishes, the needs, the lusts, the hungers, of everyone, and only one person stood in the way and that was Kino, so that he became curiously every man's enemy. The news stirred up something infinitely black and evil in the town; the black distillate was like the scorpion, or like hunger in the smell of food, or like loneliness when love is withheld. The poison sacs of the town began to manufacture venom, and the town swelled and puffed with the pressure of it.

But Kino and Juana did not know these things. Because they were happy and excited they thought everyone shared their joy. Juan Tomás and Apolonia did, and they were the world too. In the afternoon, when the sun had gone over the mountains of the Peninsula to sink in the outward sea, Kino squatted in his house with Juana beside him. And the brush house was crowded with neighbors. Kino held the great pearl in his hand, and it was warm and alive in his hand. And the music of the pearl had merged with the music of the family so that one beautified the other. The neighbors looked at the pearl in Kino's hand and they wondered how such luck could come to any man.

And Juan Tomás, who squatted on Kino's right hand because he was his brother, asked, "What will you do now that you have become a rich man?"

Kino looked into his pearl, and Juana cast her eyelashes down and arranged her shawl to cover her face so that her excitement could not be seen. And in the incandescence of the pearl the pictures formed of the things Kino's mind had considered in the past and had given up as impossible. In the pearl he saw Juana and Coyotito and himself standing and kneeling at the high altar, and they were being married now that they could pay. He spoke softly, "We will be married—in the church."

In the pearl he saw how they were dressed—Juana in a shawl stiff with newness and a new skirt, and from under the long skirt Kino could see that she wore shoes. It was in the pearl—the picture glowing there. He himself was dressed in new white clothes, and he carried a new hat— not of straw but of fine black felt—and he too wore shoes— not sandals but shoes that laced. But Coyotito—he was the one—he wore a blue sailor suit from the United States and a little yachting cap such as Kino had seen once when a pleasure boat put into the estuary. All of these things Kino saw in the lucent pearl and he said, "We will have new clothes."

And the music of the pearl rose like a chorus of trumpets in his ears.

Then to the lovely gray surface of the pearl came the little things Kino wanted: a harpoon to take the place of one lost a year ago, a new harpoon of iron with a ring in the end of the shaft; and—his mind could hardly make the leap—a rifle—but why not, since he was so rich. And Kino saw Kino in the pearl, Kino holding a Winchester carbine. It was the wildest daydreaming and very pleasant. His lips moved hesitantly over this—"A rifle," he said. "Perhaps a rifle."

It was the rifle that broke down the barriers. This was an impossibility, and if he could think of having a rifle whole horizons were burst and he could rush on. For it is said that humans are never satisfied, that you give them one thing and they want something more. And this is said in disparagement, whereas it is one of the greatest talents the species has and one that has made it superior to animals that are satisfied with what they have.

The neighbors, close pressed and silent in the house, nodded their heads at his wild imaginings. And a man in the rear murmured, "A rifle. He will have a rifle."

But the music of the pearl was shrilling with triumph in Kino. Juana looked up, and her eyes were wide at Kino's courage and at his imagination. And electric strength had come to him now the horizons were kicked out. In the pearl he saw Coyotito sitting at a little desk in a school, just as Kino had once seen it through an open door. And Coyotito was dressed in a jacket, and he had on a white collar and a broad silken tie. Moreover, Coyotito was writing on a big piece of paper. Kino looked at his neighbors fiercely. "My son will go to school," he said, and the neighbors were hushed. Juana caught her breath sharply. Her eyes were bright as she watched him, and she looked quickly down at Coyotito in her arms to see whether this might be possible.

But Kino's face shone with prophecy. "My son will read and open the books, and my son will write and will know writing. And my son will make numbers, and these things will make us free because he will know—he will know and through him we will know." And in the pearl Kino saw himself and Juana squatting by the little fire in the brush hut while Coyotito read from a great book. "This is what the pearl will do," said Kino. And he had never said so many words together in his life. And suddenly he was afraid of his talking. His hand closed down over the pearl and cut the light away from it. Kino was afraid as a man is afraid who says, "I will," without knowing.

Now the neighbors knew they had witnessed a great marvel. They knew that time would now date from Kino's pearl, and that they would discuss this moment for many years to come. If these things came to pass, they would recount how Kino looked and what he said and how his eyes shone, and they would say, "He was a man transfigured. Some power was given to him, and there it started. You see what a great man he has become, starting from that moment. And I myself saw it."

And if Kino's planning came to nothing, those same neighbors would say, "There it started. A foolish madness came over him so that he spoke foolish words. God keep us from such things. Yes, God punished Kino because he rebelled against the way things are. You see what has become of him. And I myself saw the moment when his reason left him."

Kino looked down at his closed hand and the knuckles were scabbed over and tight where he had struck the gate.

Now the dusk was coming. And Juana looped her shawl under the baby so that he hung against her hip, and she went to the fire hole and dug a coal from the ashes and broke a few twigs over it and fanned a flame alive. The little flames danced on the faces of the neighbors. They knew they should go to their own dinners, but they were reluctant to leave.

The dark was almost in, and Juana's fire threw shadows on the brush walls when the whisper came in, passed from mouth to mouth. "The Father is coming—the priest is coming." The men uncovered their heads and stepped back from the door, and the women gathered their shawls about their faces and cast down their eyes. Kino and Juan Tomás, his brother, stood up. The priest came in—a graying, aging man with an old skin and a young sharp eye. Children, he considered these people, and he treated them like children.

"Kino," he said softly, "thou art named after a great man—and a great Father of the Church." He made it sound like a benediction. "Thy namesake tamed the desert and sweetened the minds of thy people, didst thou know that? It is in the books."

Kino looked quickly down at Coyotito's head, where he hung on Juana's hip. Some day, his mind said, that boy would know what things were in the books and what things were not. The music had gone out of Kino's head, but now, thinly, slowly, the melody of the morning, the music of evil, of the enemy sounded, but it was faint and weak. And Kino looked at his neighbors to see who might have brought this song in.

But the priest was speaking again. "It has come to me that thou hast found a great fortune, a great pearl."

Kino opened his hand and held it out, and the priest gasped a little at the size and beauty of the pearl. And then he said, "I hope thou wilt remember to give thanks, my son, to Him who has given thee this treasure, and to pray for guidance in the future."

Kino nodded dumbly, and it was Juana who spoke softly. "We will, Father. And we will be married now. Kino has said so." She looked at the neighbors for confirmation, and they nodded their heads solemnly.

The priest said, "It is pleasant to see that your first thoughts are good thoughts. God bless you, my children." He turned and left quietly, and the people let him through.

But Kino's hand had closed tightly on the pearl again,

and he was glancing about suspiciously, for the evil song was in his ears, shrilling against the music of the pearl.

The neighbors slipped away to go to their houses, and Juana squatted by the fire and set her clay pot of boiled beans over the little flame. Kino stepped to the doorway and looked out. As always, he could smell the smoke from many fires, and he could see the hazy stars and feel the damp of the night air so that he covered his nose from it. The thin dog came to him and threshed itself in greeting like a windblown flag, and Kino looked down at it and didn't see it. He had broken through the horizons into a cold and lonely outside. He felt alone and unprotected, and scraping crickets and shrilling tree frogs and croaking toads seemed to be carrying the melody of evil. Kino shivered a little and drew his blanket more tightly against his nose. He carried the pearl still in his hand, tightly closed in his palm, and it was warm and smooth against his skin.

Behind him he heard Juana patting the cakes before she put them down on the clay cooking sheet. Kino felt all the warmth and security of his family behind him, and the Song of the Family came from behind him like the purring of a kitten. But now, by saying what his future was going to be like, he had created it. A plan is a real thing, and things projected are experienced. A plan once made and visualized becomes a reality along with other realities—never to be destroyed but easily to be attacked. Thus Kino's future was real, but having set it up, other forces were set up to destroy it, and this he knew, so that he had to prepare to meet the attack. And this Kino knew also—that the gods do not love men's plans, and the gods do not love success unless it comes by accident. He knew that the gods take their revenge on a man if he be successful through his own efforts. Consequently Kino was afraid of plans, but having made one, he could never destroy it. And to meet the attack, Kino was already making a hard skin for himself against the world. His eyes and his mind probed for danger before it appeared.

Standing in the door, he saw two men approach; and one of them carried a lantern which lighted the ground and the legs of the men. They turned in through the opening of Kino's brush fence and came to his door. And Kino saw that one was the doctor and the other the servant who had opened the gate in the morning. The split knuckles on Kino's right hand burned when he saw who they were.

The doctor said, "I was not in when you came this morning. But now, at the first chance, I have come to see the baby."

Kino stood in the door, filling it, and hatred raged and flamed in the back of his eyes, and fear too, for the hundreds of years of subjugation were cut deep in him.

"The baby is nearly well now," he said curtly.

The doctor smiled, but his eyes in their little lymphlined hammocks did not smile.

He said, "Sometimes, my friend, the scorpion sting has a curious effect. There will be apparent improvement, and then without warning—pouf!" He pursed his lips and made a little explosion to show how quick it could be, and he shifted his small black doctor's bag about so that the light of the lamp fell upon it, for he knew that Kino's race love the tools of any craft and trust them. "Sometimes," the doctor went on in a liquid tone, "sometimes there will be a withered leg or a blind eye or a crumpled back. Oh, I know the sting of the scorpion, my friend, and I can cure it."

Kino felt the rage and hatred melting toward fear. He

did not know, and perhaps this doctor did. And he could not take the chance of pitting his certain ignorance against this man's possible knowledge. He was trapped as his people were always trapped, and would be until, as he had said, they could be sure that the things in the books were really in the books. He could not take a chance—not with the life or with the straightness of Coyotito. He stood aside and let the doctor and his man enter the brush hut.

Juana stood up from the fire and backed away as he entered, and she covered the baby's face with the fringe of her shawl. And when the doctor went to her and held out his hand, she clutched the baby tight and looked at Kino where he stood with the fire shadows leaping on his face.

Kino nodded, and only then did she let the doctor take the baby.

"Hold the light," the doctor said, and when the servant held the lantern high, the doctor looked for a moment at the wound on the baby's shoulder. He was thoughtful for a moment and then he rolled back the baby's eyelid and looked at the eyeball. He nodded his head while Coyotito struggled against him.

"It is as I thought," he said. "The poison has gone inward and it will strike soon. Come look!" He held the eyelid down. "See—it is blue." And Kino, looking anxiously, saw that indeed it was a little blue. And he didn't know whether or not it was always a little blue. But the trap was set. He couldn't take the chance.

The doctor's eyes watered in their little hammocks. "I will give him something to try to turn the poison aside," he said. And he handed the baby to Kino.

Then from his bag he took a little bottle of white powder and a capsule of gelatine. He filled the capsule with the powder and closed it, and then around the first capsule he fitted a second capsule and closed it. Then he worked very deftly. He took the baby and pinched its lower lip until it opened its mouth. His fat fingers placed the capsule far back on the baby's tongue, back of the point where he could spit it out, and then from the floor he picked up the little pitcher of pulque and gave Coyotito a drink, and it was done. He looked again at the baby's eyeball and he pursed his lips and seemed to think.

At last he handed the baby back to Juana, and he turned to Kino. "I think the poison will attack within the hour," he said. "The medicine may save the baby from hurt, but I will come back in an hour. Perhaps I am in time to save him." He took a deep breath and went out of the hut, and his servant followed him with the lantern.

Now Juana had the baby under her shawl, and she stared at it with anxiety and fear. Kino came to her, and he lifted the shawl and stared at the baby. He moved his hand to look under the eyelid, and only then saw that the pearl was still in his hand. Then he went to a box by the wall, and from it he brought a piece of rag. He wrapped the pearl in the rag, then went to the corner of the brush house and dug a little hole with his fingers in the dirt floor, and he put the pearl in the hole and covered it up and concealed the place. And then he went to the fire where Juana was squatting, watching the baby's face.

The doctor, back in his house, settled into his chair and looked at his watch. His people brought him a little supper of chocolate and sweet cakes and fruit, and he stared at the food discontentedly.

In the houses of the neighbors the subject that would lead all conversations for a long time to come was aired for the first time to see how it would go. The neighbors showed one another with their thumbs how big the pearl was, and they made little caressing gestures to show how lovely it was. From now on they would watch Kino and Juana very closely to see whether riches turned their heads, as riches turn all people's heads. Everyone knew why the doctor had come. He was not good at dissembling and he was very well understood.

Out in the estuary a tight woven school of small fishes glittered and broke water to escape a school of great fishes that drove in to eat them. And in the houses the people could hear the swish of the small ones and the bouncing splash of the great ones as the slaughter went on. The dampness arose out of the Gulf and was deposited on bushes and cacti and on little trees in salty drops. And the night mice crept about on the ground and the little night hawks hunted them silently.

The skinny black puppy with flame spots over his eyes came to Kino's door and looked in. He nearly shook his hind quarters loose when Kino glanced up at him, and he subsided when Kino looked away. The puppy did not enter the house, but he watched with frantic interest while Kino ate his beans from the little pottery dish and wiped it clean with a corncake and ate the cake and washed the whole down with a drink of pulque.

Kino was finished and was rolling a cigarette when Juana spoke sharply. "Kino." He glanced at her and then got up and went quickly to her for he saw fright in her eyes. He stood over her, looking down, but the light was very dim. He kicked a pile of twigs into the fire hole to make a blaze, and then he could see the face of Coyotito. The baby's face was flushed and his throat was working and a little thick drool of saliva issued from his lips. The spasm of the stomach muscles began, and the baby was very sick.

Kino knelt beside his wife. "So the doctor knew," he said, but he said it for himself as well as for his wife, for his mind was hard and suspicious and he was remembering the white powder. Juana rocked from side to side and moaned out the little Song of the Family as though it could ward off the danger, and the baby vomited and writhed in her arms. Now uncertainty was in Kino, and the music of evil throbbed in his head and nearly drove out Juana's song.

The doctor finished his chocolate and nibbled the little fallen pieces of sweet cake. He brushed his fingers on a napkin, looked at his watch, arose, and took up his little bag.

The news of the baby's illness traveled quickly among the brush houses, for sickness is second only to hunger as the enemy of poor people. And some said softly, "Luck, you see, brings bitter friends." And they nodded and got up to go to Kino's house. The neighbors scuttled with covered noses through the dark until they crowded into Kino's house again. They stood and gazed, and they made little comments on the sadness that this should happen at a time of joy, and they said, "All things are in God's hands." The old women squatted down beside Juana to try to give her aid if they could and comfort if they could not.

Then the doctor hurried in, followed by his man. He scattered the old women like chickens. He took the baby and examined it and felt its head. "The poison it has worked," he said. "I think I can defeat it. I will try my best." He asked for water, and in the cup of it he put three drops of ammonia, and he pried open the baby's mouth and poured it down. The baby spluttered and screeched under the treatment, and Juana watched him with haunted eyes. The doctor spoke a little as he worked. "It is lucky that I know about the poison of the scorpion, otherwise—" and he shrugged to show what could have happened.

But Kino was suspicious, and he could not take his eyes from the doctor's open bag, and from the bottle of white powder there. Gradually the spasms subsided and the baby relaxed under the doctor's hands. And then Coyotito sighed deeply and went to sleep, for he was very tired with vomiting.

The doctor put the baby in Juana's arms. "He will get well now," he said. "I have won the fight." And Juana looked at him with adoration.

The doctor was closing his bag now. He said, "When do you think you can pay this bill?" He said it even kindly.

"When I have sold my pearl I will pay you," Kino said.

"You have a pearl? A good pearl?" the doctor asked with interest.

And then the chorus of the neighbors broke in. "He has found the Pearl of the World," they cried, and they joined forefinger with thumb to show how great the pearl was.

"Kino will be a rich man," they clamored. "It is a pearl such as one has never seen."

The doctor looked surprised. "I had not heard of it. Do you keep this pearl in a safe place? Perhaps you would like me to put it in my safe?"

Kino's eyes were hooded now, his cheeks were drawn taut. "I have it secure," he said. "Tomorrow I will sell it and then I will pay you."

The doctor shrugged, and his wet eyes never left Kino's eyes. He knew the pearl would be buried in the house, and he thought Kino might look toward the place where it was buried. "It would be a shame to have it stolen before you could sell it," the doctor said, and he saw Kino's eyes flick involuntarily to the floor near the side post of the brush house.

When the doctor had gone and all the neighbors had reluctantly returned to their houses, Kino squatted beside the little glowing coals in the fire hole and listened to the night sound, the soft sweep of the little waves on the shore and the distant barking of dogs, the creeping of the breeze through the brush house roof and the soft speech of his neighbors in their houses in the village. For these people do not sleep soundly all night; they awaken at intervals and talk a little and then go to sleep again. And after a while Kino got up and went to the door of his house.

He smelled the breeze and he listened for any foreign sound of secrecy or creeping, and his eyes searched the darkness, for the music of evil was sounding in his head and he was fierce and afraid. After he had probed the night with his senses he went to the place by the side post where the pearl was buried, and he dug it up and brought it to his sleeping mat, and under his sleeping mat he dug another little hole in the dirt floor and buried the pearl and covered it up again.

And Juana, sitting by the fire hole, watched him with questioning eyes, and when he had buried his pearl she asked, "Who do you fear?"

Kino searched for a true answer, and at last he said, "Everyone." And he could feel a shell of hardness drawing over him.

After a while they lay down together on the sleeping mat, and Juana did not put the baby in his box tonight, but cradled him in her arms and covered his face with her head shawl. And the last light went out of the embers in the fire hole.

But Kino's brain burned, even during his sleep, and he dreamed that Coyotito could read, that one of his own people could tell him the truth of things. And in his dream, Coyotito was reading from a book as large as a house, with letters as big as dogs, and the words galloped and played on the book. And then darkness spread over the page, and with the darkness came the music of evil again, and Kino stirred in his sleep; and when he stirred, Juana's eyes opened in the darkness. And then Kino awakened, with the evil music pulsing in him, and he lay in the darkness with his ears alert.

Then from the corner of the house came a sound so soft that it might have been simply a thought, a little furtive movement, a touch of a foot on earth, the almost inaudible purr of controlled breathing. Kino held his breath to listen, and he knew that whatever dark thing was in his house was holding its breath too, to listen. For a time no sound at all came from the corner of the brush house. Then Kino might have thought he had imagined the sound. But Juana's hand came creeping over to him in warning, and then the sound came again! the whisper of a foot on dry earth and the scratch of fingers in the soil.

And now a wild fear surged in Kino's breast, and on the fear came rage, as it always did. Kino's hand crept into his breast where his knife hung on a string, and then he sprang like an angry cat, leaped striking and spitting for the dark thing he knew was in the corner of the house. He felt cloth, struck at it with his knife and missed, and struck again and felt his knife go through cloth, and then his head crashed with lightning and exploded with pain. There was a soft scurry in the doorway, and running steps for a moment, and then silence.

Kino could feel warm blood running from his forehead, and he could hear Juana calling to him. "Kino! Kino!" And there was terror in her voice. Then coldness came over him as quickly as the rage had, and he said, "I am all right. The thing has gone."

He groped his way back to the sleeping mat. Already Juana was working at the fire. She uncovered an ember from the ashes and shredded little pieces of cornhusk over it and blew a little flame into the cornhusks so that a tiny light danced through the hut. And then from a secret place Juana brought a little piece of consecrated candle and lighted it at the flame and set it upright on a fireplace stone. She worked quickly, crooning as she moved about. She dipped the end of her head shawl in water and swabbed the blood from Kino's bruised forehead. "It is nothing," Kino said, but his eyes and his voice were hard and cold and a brooding hate was growing in him.

Now the tension which had been growing in Juana boiled up to the surface and her lips were thin. "This thing is evil," she cried harshly. "This pearl is like a sin! It will destroy us," and her voice rose shrilly. "Throw it away, Kino. Let us break it between stones. Let us bury it and forget the place. Let us throw it back into the sea. It has brought evil. Kino, my husband, it will destroy us." And in the firelight her lips and her eyes were alive with her fear.

But Kino's face was set, and his mind and his will were set. "This is our one chance," he said. "Our son must go to school. He must break out of the pot that holds us in."

"It will destroy us all," Juana cried. "Even our son."

"Hush," said Kino. "Do not speak any more. In the

morning we will sell the pearl, and then the evil will be gone, and only the good remain. Now hush, my wife." His dark eyes scowled into the little fire, and for the first time he knew that his knife was still in his hands, and he raised the blade and looked at it and saw a little line of blood on the steel. For a moment he seemed about to wipe the blade on his trousers but then he plunged the knife into the earth and so cleansed it.

The distant roosters began to crow and the air changed and the dawn was coming. The wind of the morning ruffled the water of the estuary and whispered through the mangroves, and the little waves beat on the rubbly beach with an increased tempo. Kino raised the sleeping mat and dug up his pearl and put it in front of him and stared at it.

And the beauty of the pearl, winking and glimmering in the light of the little candle, cozened his brain with its beauty. So lovely it was, so soft, and its own music came from it—its music of promise and delight, its guarantee of the future, of comfort, of security. Its warm lucence promised a poultice against illness and a wall against insult. It closed a door on hunger. And as he stared at it Kino's eyes softened and his face relaxed. He could see the little image of the consecrated candle reflected in the soft surface of the pearl, and he heard again in his ears the lovely music of the undersea, the tone of the diffused green light of the sea bottom. Juana, glancing secretly at him, saw him smile. And because they were in some way one thing and one purpose, she smiled with him.

And they began this day with hope.

4

It is wonderful the way a little town keeps track of itself and of all its units. If every single man and woman, child and baby, acts and conducts itself in a known pattern and breaks no walls and differs with no one and experiments in no way and is not sick and does not endanger the ease and peace of mind or steady unbroken flow of the town, then that unit can disappear and never be heard of. But let one man step out of the regular thought or the known and trusted pattern, and the nerves of the townspeople ring with nervousness and communication travels over the nerve lines of the town. Then every unit communicates to the whole.

Thus, in La Paz, it was known in the early morning through the whole town that Kino was going to sell his pearl that day. It was known among the neighbors in the brush huts, among the pearl fishermen; it was known among the Chinese grocery-store owners; it was known in the church, for the altar boys whispered about it. Word of it crept in among the nuns; the beggars in front of the church spoke of it, for they would be there to take the tithe of the first fruits of the luck. The little boys knew about it with excitement, but most of all the pearl buyers knew about it, and when the day had come, in the offices of the pearl buyers, each man sat alone with his little black velvet tray, and each man rolled the pearls about with his fingertips and considered his part in the picture.

It was supposed that the pearl buyers were individuals acting alone, bidding against one another for the pearls the fishermen brought in. And once it had been so. But this was a wasteful method, for often, in the excitement of bidding for a fine pearl, too great a price had been paid to the fishermen. This was extravagant and not to be countenanced. Now there was only one pearl buyer with many hands, and the men who sat in their offices and waited for Kino knew what price they would offer, how high they would bid, and what method each one would use. And although these men would not profit beyond their salaries, there was excitement among the pearl buyers, for there was excitement in the hunt, and if it be a man's function to break down a price, then he must take joy and satisfaction in breaking it as far down as possible. For every man in the world functions to the best of his ability, and no one does less than his best, no matter what he may think about it. Quite apart from any reward they might get, from any word of praise, from any promotion, a pearl buyer was a pearl buyer, and the best and happiest pearl buyer was he who bought for the lowest prices.

The sun was hot yellow that morning, and it drew the moisture from the estuary and from the Gulf and hung it in shimmering scarves in the air so that the air vibrated and vision was insubstantial. A vision hung in the air to the north of the city—the vision of a mountain that was over two hundred miles away, and the high slopes of this mountain were swaddled with pines and a great stone peak arose above the timber line.

And the morning of this day the canoes lay lined up on the beach; the fishermen did not go out to dive for pearls, for there would be too much happening, too many things to see when Kino went to sell the great pearl.

In the brush houses by the shore Kino's neighbors sat long over their breakfasts, and they spoke of what they would do if they had found the pearl. And one man said that he would give it as a present to the Holy Father in Rome. Another said that he would buy Masses for the souls of his family for a thousand years. Another thought he might take the money and distribute it among the poor of La Paz; and a fourth thought of all the good things one could do with the money from the pearl, of all the charities, benefits, of all the rescues one could perform if one had money. All of the neighbors hoped that sudden wealth would not turn Kino's head, would not make a rich man of him, would not graft onto him the evil limbs of greed and hatred and coldness. For Kino was a well-liked man; it would be a shame if the pearl destroyed him. "That good wife Juana," they said, "and the beautiful baby Coyotito, and the others to come. What a pity it would be if the pearl should destroy them all."

For Kino and Juana this was the morning of mornings of their lives, comparable only to the day when the baby had been born. This was to be the day from which all other days would take their arrangement. Thus they would say, "It was two years before we sold the pearl," or, "It was six weeks after we sold the pearl." Juana, considering the matter, threw caution to the winds, and she dressed Coyotito in the clothes she had prepared for his baptism, when there would be money for his baptism. And Juana combed and braided her hair and tied the ends with two little bows of red ribbon, and she put on her marriage skirt and waist. The sun was quarter high when they were ready. Kino's ragged white clothes were clean at least, and this was the last day of his raggedness. For tomorrow, or even this afternoon, he would have new clothes.

The neighbors, watching Kino's door through the crevices in their brush houses, were dressed and ready too. There was no self-consciousness about their joining Kino and Juana to go pearl selling. It was expected, it was an historic moment, they would be crazy if they didn't go. It would be almost a sign of unfriendship.

Juana put on her head shawl carefully, and she draped one long end under her right elbow and gathered it with her right hand so that a hammock hung under her arm, and in this little hammock she placed Coyotito, propped up against the head shawl so that he could see everything and perhaps remember. Kino put on his large straw hat and felt it with his hand to see that it was properly placed, not on the back or side of his head, like a rash, unmarried, irresponsible man, and not flat as an elder would wear it, but tilted a little forward to show aggressiveness and seriousness and vigor. There is a great deal to be seen in the tilt of a hat on a man. Kino slipped his feet into his sandals and pulled the thongs up over his heels. The great pearl was wrapped in an old soft piece of deerskin and placed in a little leather bag, and the leather bag was in a pocket in Kino's shirt. He folded his blanket carefully and draped it in a narrow strip over his left shoulder, and now they were ready.

Kino stepped with dignity out of the house, and Juana followed him, carrying Coyotito. And as they marched up the freshet-washed alley toward the town, the neighbors joined them. The houses belched people; the doorways spewed out children. But because of the seriousness of the occasion, only one man walked with Kino, and that was his brother, Juan Tomás.

Juan Tomás cautioned his brother. "You must be careful to see they do not cheat you," he said.

And, "Very careful," Kino agreed.

"We do not know what prices are paid in other places," said Juan Tomás. "How can we know what is a fair price, if we do not know what the pearl buyer gets for the pearl in another place."

"That is true," said Kino, "but how can we know? We are here, we are not there."

As they walked up toward the city the crowd grew behind them, and Juan Tomás, in pure nervousness, went on speaking.

"Before you were born, Kino," he said, "the old ones thought of a way to get more money for their pearls. They thought it would be better if they had an agent who took all the pearls to the capital and sold them there and kept only his share of the profit."

Kino nodded his head. "I know," he said. "It was a good thought."

"And so they got such a man," said Juan Tomás, "and they pooled their pearls, and they started him off. And he was never heard of again and the pearls were lost. Then they got another man, and they started him off, and he was never heard of again. And so they gave the whole thing up and went back to the old way."

"I know," said Kino. "I have heard our father tell of it. It was a good idea, but it was against religion, and the Father made that very clear. The loss of the pearl was a punishment visited on those who tried to leave their station. And the

Father made it clear that each man and woman is like a soldier sent by God to guard some part of the castle of the Universe. And some are in the ramparts and some far deep in the darkness of the walls. But each one must remain faithful to his post and must not go running about, else the castle is in danger from the assaults of Hell."

"I have heard him make that sermon," said Juan Tomás. "He makes it every year."

The brothers, as they walked along, squinted their eyes a little, as they and their grandfathers and their greatgrandfathers had done for four hundred years, since first the strangers came with argument and authority and gunpowder to back up both. And in the four hundred years Kino's people had learned only one defense—a slight slitting of the eyes and a slight tightening of the lips and a retirement. Nothing could break down this wall, and they could remain whole within the wall.

The gathering procession was solemn, for they sensed the importance of this day, and any children who showed a tendency to scuffle, to scream, to cry out, to steal hats and rumple hair, were hissed to silence by their elders. So important was this day that an old man came to see, riding on the stalwart shoulders of his nephew. The procession left the brush huts and entered the stone and plaster city where the streets were a little wider and there were narrow pavements beside the buildings. And as before, the beggars joined them as they passed the church; the grocers looked out at them as they went by; the little saloons lost their customers and the owners closed up shop and went along. And the sun beat down on the streets of the city and even tiny stones threw shadows on the ground.

The news of the approach of the procession ran ahead of

it, and in their little dark offices the pearl buyers stiffened and grew alert. They got out papers so that they could be at work when Kino appeared, and they put their pearls in the desks, for it is not good to let an inferior pearl be seen beside a beauty. And word of the loveliness of Kino's pearl had come to them. The pearl buyers' offices were clustered together in one narrow street, and they were barred at the windows, and wooden slats cut out the light so that only a soft gloom entered the offices.

A stout slow man sat in an office waiting. His face was fatherly and benign, and his eyes twinkled with friendship. He was a caller of good mornings, a ceremonious shaker of hands, a jolly man who knew all jokes and yet who hovered close to sadness, for in the midst of a laugh he could remember the death of your aunt, and his eyes could become wet with sorrow for your loss. This morning he had placed a flower in a vase on his desk, a single scarlet hibiscus, and the vase sat beside the black velvet-lined pearl tray in front of him. He was shaved close to the blue roots of his beard, and his hands were clean and his nails polished. His door stood open to the morning, and he hummed under his breath while his right hand practiced legerdemain. He rolled a coin back and forth over his knuckles and made it appear and disappear, made it spin and sparkle. The coin winked into sight and as quickly slipped out of sight, and the man did not even watch his own performance. The fingers did it all mechanically, precisely, while the man hummed to himself and peered out the door. Then he heard the tramp of feet of the approaching crowd, and the fingers of his right hand worked faster and faster until, as the figure of Kino filled the doorway, the coin flashed and disappeared.

"Good morning, my friend," the stout man said. "What can I do for you?"

Kino stared into the dimness of the little office, for his eyes were squeezed from the outside glare. But the buyer's eyes had become as steady and cruel and unwinking as a hawk's eyes, while the rest of his face smiled in greeting. And secretly, behind his desk, his right hand practiced with the coin.

"I have a pearl," said Kino. And Juan Tomás stood beside him and snorted a little at the understatement. The neighbors peered around the doorway, and a line of little boys clambered on the window bars and looked through. Several little boys, on their hands and knees, watched the scene around Kino's legs.

"You have a pearl," the dealer said. "Sometimes a man brings in a dozen. Well, let us see your pearl. We will value it and give you the best price." And his fingers worked furiously with the coin.

Now Kino instinctively knew his own dramatic effects. Slowly he brought out the leather bag, slowly took from it the soft and dirty piece of deerskin, and then he let the great pearl roll into the black velvet tray, and instantly his eyes went to the buyer's face. But there was no sign, no movement, the face did not change, but the secret hand behind the desk missed in its precision. The coin stumbled over a knuckle and slipped silently into the dealer's lap. And the fingers behind the desk curled into a fist. When the right hand came out of hiding, the forefinger touched the great pearl, rolled it on the black velvet; thumb and forefinger picked it up and brought it near to the dealer's eyes and twirled it in the air.

Kino held his breath, and the neighbors held their breath,

and the whispering went back through the crowd. "He is inspecting it—No price has been mentioned yet—They have not come to a price."

Now the dealer's hand had become a personality. The hand tossed the great pearl back in the tray, the forefinger poked and insulted it, and on the dealer's face there came a sad and contemptuous smile.

"I am sorry, my friend," he said, and his shoulders rose a little to indicate that the misfortune was no fault of his.

"It is a pearl of great value," Kino said.

The dealer's fingers spurned the pearl so that it bounced and rebounded softly from the side of the velvet tray.

"You have heard of fool's gold," the dealer said. "This pearl is like fool's gold. It is too large. Who would buy it? There is no market for such things. It is a curiosity only. I am sorry. You thought it was a thing of value, and it is only a curiosity."

Now Kino's face was perplexed and worried. "It is the Pearl of the World," he cried. "No one has ever seen such a pearl."

"On the contrary," said the dealer, "it is large and clumsy. As a curiosity it has interest; some museum might perhaps take it to place in a collection of seashells. I can give you, say, a thousand pesos."

Kino's face grew dark and dangerous. "It is worth fifty thousand," he said. "You know it. You want to cheat me."

And the dealer heard a little grumble go through the crowd as they heard his price. And the dealer felt a little tremor of fear.

"Do not blame me," he said quickly. "I am only an appraiser. Ask the others. Go to their offices and show your pearl—or better let them come here, so that you can see there is no collusion. Boy," he called. And when his servant looked through the rear door, "Boy, go to such a one, and such another one and such a third one. Ask them to step in here and do not tell them why. Just say that I will be pleased to see them." And his right hand went behind the desk and pulled another coin from his pocket, and the coin rolled back and forth over the knuckles.

Kino's neighbors whispered together. They had been afraid of something like this. The pearl was large, but it had a strange color. They had been suspicious of it from the first. And after all, a thousand pesos was not to be thrown away. It was comparative wealth to a man who was not wealthy. And suppose Kino took a thousand pesos. Only yesterday he had nothing.

But Kino had grown tight and hard. He felt the creeping of fate, the circling of wolves, the hover of vultures. He felt the evil coagulating about him, and he was helpless to protect himself. He heard in his ears the evil music. And on the black velvet the great pearl glistened, so that the dealer could not keep his eyes from it.

The crowd in the doorway wavered and broke and let the three pearl dealers through. The crowd was silent now, fearing to miss a word, to fail to see a gesture or an expression. Kino was silent and watchful. He felt a little tugging at his back, and he turned and looked in Juana's eyes, and when he looked away he had renewed strength.

The dealers did not glance at one another nor at the pearl. The man behind the desk said, "I have put a value on this pearl. The owner here does not think it fair. I will ask you to examine this—this thing and make an offer. Notice," he said to Kino, "I have not mentioned what I have offered."

The first dealer, dry and stringy, seemed now to see the pearl for the first time. He took it up, rolled it quickly between thumb and forefinger, and then cast it contemptuously back into the tray.

"Do not include me in the discussion," he said dryly. "I will make no offer at all. I do not want it. This is not a pearl—it is a monstrosity." His thin lips curled.

Now the second dealer, a little man with a shy soft voice, took up the pearl, and he examined it carefully. He took a glass from his pocket and inspected it under magnification. Then he laughed softly.

"Better pearls are made of paste," he said. "I know these things. This is soft and chalky, it will lose its color and die in a few months. Look—." He offered the glass to Kino, showed him how to use it, and Kino, who had never seen a pearl's surface magnified, was shocked at the strange-looking surface.

The third dealer took the pearl from Kino's hands. "One of my clients likes such things," he said. "I will offer five hundred pesos, and perhaps I can sell it to my client for six hundred."

Kino reached quickly and snatched the pearl from his hand. He wrapped it in the deerskin and thrust it inside his shirt.

The man behind the desk said, "I'm a fool, I know, but my first offer stands. I still offer one thousand. What are you doing?" he asked, as Kino thrust the pearl out of sight.

"I am cheated," Kino cried fiercely. "My pearl is not for sale here. I will go, perhaps even to the capital."

Now the dealers glanced quickly at one another. They knew they had played too hard; they knew they would be disciplined for their failure, and the man at the desk said quickly, "I might go to fifteen hundred."

But Kino was pushing his way through the crowd. The hum of talk came to him dimly, his rage blood pounded in his ears, and he burst through and strode away. Juana followed, trotting after him.

When the evening came, the neighbors in the brush houses sat eating their corncakes and beans, and they discussed the great theme of the morning. They did not know, it seemed a fine pearl to them, but they had never seen such a pearl before, and surely the dealers knew more about the value of pearls than they. "And mark this," they said. "Those dealers did not discuss these things. Each of the three knew the pearl was valueless."

"But suppose they had arranged it before?"

"If that is so, then all of us have been cheated all of our lives."

Perhaps, some argued, perhaps it would have been better if Kino took the one thousand five hundred pesos. That is a great deal of money, more than he has ever seen. Maybe Kino is being a pigheaded fool. Suppose he should really go to the capital and find no buyer for his pearl. He would never live that down.

And now, said other fearful ones, now that he had defied them, those buyers will not want to deal with him at all. Maybe Kino has cut off his own head and destroyed himself.

And others said, Kino is a brave man, and a fierce man; he is right. From his courage we may all profit. These were proud of Kino.

In his house Kino squatted on his sleeping mat, brooding. He had buried his pearl under a stone of the fire hole in his house, and he stared at the woven tules of his sleeping mat until the crossed design danced in his head. He had lost one world and had not gained another. And Kino was afraid. Never in his life had he been far from home. He was afraid of strangers and of strange places. He was terrified of that monster of strangeness they called the capital. It lay over the water and through the mountains, over a thousand miles, and every strange terrible mile was frightening. But Kino had lost his old world and he must clamber on to a new one. For his dream of the future was real and never to be destroyed, and he had said "I will go," and that made a real thing too. To determine to go and to say it was to be halfway there.

Juana watched him while he buried his pearl, and she watched him while she cleaned Coyotito and nursed him, and Juana made the corncakes for supper.

Juan Tomás came in and squatted down beside Kino and remained silent for a long time, until at last Kino demanded, "What else could I do? They are cheats."

Juan Tomás nodded gravely. He was the elder, and Kino looked to him for wisdom. "It is hard to know," he said. "We do know that we are cheated from birth to the overcharge on our coffins. But we survive. You have defied not the pearl buyers, but the whole structure, the whole way of life, and I am afraid for you."

"What have I to fear but starvation?" Kino asked.

But Juan Tomás shook his head slowly. "That we must all fear. But suppose you are correct—suppose your pearl is of great value—do you think then the game is over?"

"What do you mean?"

"I don't know," said Juan Tomás, "but I am afraid for you. It is new ground you are walking on, you do not know the way."

"I will go. I will go soon," said Kino.

"Yes," Juan Tomás agreed. "That you must do. But I wonder if you will find it any different in the capital. Here, you have friends and me, your brother. There, you will have no one."

"What can I do?" Kino cried. "Some deep outrage is here. My son must have a chance. That is what they are striking at. My friends will protect me."

"Only so long as they are not in danger or discomfort from it," said Juan Tomás. He arose, saying, "Go with God."

And Kino said, "Go with God," and did not even look up, for the words had a strange chill in them.

Long after Juan Tomás had gone Kino sat brooding on his sleeping mat. A lethargy had settled on him, and a little gray hopelessness. Every road seemed blocked against him. In his head he heard only the dark music of the enemy. His senses were burningly alive, but his mind went back to the deep participation with all things, the gift he had from his people. He heard every little sound of the gathering night, the sleepy complaint of settling birds, the love agony of cats, the strike and withdrawal of little waves on the beach, and the simple hiss of distance. And he could smell the sharp odor of exposed kelp from the receding tide. The little flare of the twig fire made the design on his sleeping mat jump before his entranced eyes.

Juana watched him with worry, but she knew him and she knew she could help him best by being silent and by being near. And as though she too could hear the Song of Evil, she fought it, singing softly the melody of the family, of the safety and warmth and wholeness of the family. She held Coyotito in her arms and sang the song to him, to keep the evil out, and her voice was brave against the threat of the dark music.

Kino did not move nor ask for his supper. She knew he would ask when he wanted it. His eyes were entranced, and he could sense the wary, watchful evil outside the brush house; he could feel the dark creeping things waiting for him to go out into the night. It was shadowy and dreadful, and yet it called to him and threatened him and challenged him. His right hand went into his shirt and felt his knife; his eyes were wide; he stood up and walked to the doorway.

Juana willed to stop him; she raised her hand to stop him, and her mouth opened with terror. For a long moment Kino looked out into the darkness and then he stepped outside. Juana heard the little rush, the grunting struggle, the blow. She froze with terror for a moment, and then her lips drew back from her teeth like a cat's lips. She set Coyotito down on the ground. She seized a stone from the fireplace and rushed outside, but it was over by then. Kino lay on the ground, struggling to rise, and there was no one near him. Only the shadows and the strike and rush of waves and the hiss of distance. But the evil was all about, hidden behind the brush fence, crouched beside the house in the shadow, hovering in the air.

Juana dropped her stone, and she put her arms around Kino and helped him to his feet and supported him into the house. Blood oozed down from his scalp and there was a long deep cut in his cheek from ear to chin, a deep, bleeding slash. And Kino was only half conscious. He shook his head from side to side. His shirt was torn open and his clothes half pulled off. Juana sat him down on his sleeping mat and she wiped the thickening blood from his face with her skirt. She brought him pulque to drink in a little pitcher, and still he shook his head to clear out the darkness.

"Who?" Juana asked.

"I don't know," Kino said. "I didn't see."

Now Juana brought her clay pot of water and she washed the cut on his face while he stared dazed ahead of him.

"Kino, my husband," she cried, and his eyes stared past her. "Kino, can you hear me?"

"I hear you," he said dully.

"Kino, this pearl is evil. Let us destroy it before it destroys us. Let us crush it between two stones. Let us—let us throw it back in the sea where it belongs. Kino, it is evil, it is evil!"

And as she spoke the light came back in Kino's eyes so that they glowed fiercely and his muscles hardened and his will hardened.

"No," he said. "I will fight this thing. I will win over it. We will have our chance." His fist pounded the sleeping mat. "No one shall take our good fortune from us," he said. His eyes softened then and he raised a gentle hand to Juana's shoulder. "Believe me," he said. "I am a man." And his face grew crafty.

"In the morning we will take our canoe and we will go over the sea and over the mountains to the capital, you and I. We will not be cheated. I am a man."

"Kino," she said huskily, "I am afraid. A man can be killed. Let us throw the pearl back into the sea."

"Hush," he said fiercely. "I am a man. Hush." And she was silent, for his voice was command. "Let us sleep a little," he said. "In the first light we will start. You are not afraid to go with me?"

"No, my husband."

His eyes were soft and warm on her then, his hand touched her cheek. "Let us sleep a little," he said.

5

The late moon arose before the first rooster crowed. Kino opened his eyes in the darkness, for he sensed movement near him, but he did not move. Only his eyes searched the darkness, and in the pale light of the moon that crept through the holes in the brush house Kino saw Juana arise silently from beside him. He saw her move toward the fireplace. So carefully did she work that he heard only the lightest sound when she moved the fireplace stone. And then like a shadow she glided toward the door. She paused for a moment beside the hanging box where Coyotito lay, then for a second she was black in the doorway, and then she was gone.

And rage surged in Kino. He rolled up to his feet and followed her as silently as she had gone, and he could hear her quick footsteps going toward the shore. Quietly he tracked her, and his brain was red with anger. She burst clear out of the brush line and stumbled over the little boulders toward the water, and then she heard him coming and she broke into a run. Her arm was up to throw when he leaped at her and caught her arm and wrenched the pearl from her. He struck her in the face with his clenched fist and she fell among the boulders, and he kicked her in the side. In the pale light he could see the little waves break over her, and her skirt floated about and clung to her legs as the water receded.

Kino looked down at her and his teeth were bared. He hissed at her like a snake, and Juana stared at him with wide unfrightened eyes, like a sheep before the butcher. She knew there was murder in him, and it was all right; she had accepted it, and she would not resist or even protest. And then the rage left him and a sick disgust took its place. He turned away from her and walked up the beach and through the brush line. His senses were dulled by his emotion.

He heard the rush, got his knife out and lunged at one dark figure and felt his knife go home, and then he was swept to his knees and swept again to the ground. Greedy fingers went through his clothes, frantic figures searched him, and the pearl, knocked from his hand, lay winking behind a little stone in the pathway. It glinted in the soft moonlight.

Juana dragged herself up from the rocks on the edge of the water. Her face was a dull pain and her side ached. She steadied herself on her knees for a while and her wet skirt clung to her. There was no anger in her for Kino. He had said, "I am a man," and that meant certain things to Juana. It meant that he was half insane and half god. It meant that Kino would drive his strength against a mountain and plunge his strength against the sea. Juana, in her woman's soul, knew that the mountain would stand while the man broke himself; that the sea would surge while the man drowned in it. And yet it was this thing that made him a man, half insane and half god, and Juana had need of a man; she could not live without a man. Although she might be puzzled by these differences between man and woman, she knew them and accepted them and needed them. Of course

she would follow him, there was no question of that. Sometimes the quality of woman, the reason, the caution, the
sense of preservation, could cut through Kino's manness
and save them all. She climbed painfully to her feet, and
she dipped her cupped palms in the little waves and washed
her bruised face with the stinging salt water, and then she
went creeping up the beach after Kino.

A flight of herring clouds had moved over the sky from
the south. The pale moon dipped in and out of the strands
of clouds so that Juana walked in darkness for a moment
and in light the next. Her back was bent with pain and her
head was low. She went through the line of brush when the
moon was covered, and when it looked through she saw the
glimmer of the great pearl in the path behind the rock. She
sank to her knees and picked it up, and the moon went into
the darkness of the clouds again. Juana remained on her
knees while she considered whether to go back to the sea
and finish her job, and as she considered, the light came
again, and she saw two dark figures lying in the path ahead
of her. She leaped forward and saw that one was Kino and
the other a stranger with dark shiny fluid leaking from his
throat.

Kino moved sluggishly, arms and legs stirred like those
of a crushed bug, and a thick muttering came from his
mouth. Now, in an instant, Juana knew that the old life was
gone forever. A dead man in the path and Kino's knife, dark
bladed beside him, convinced her. All of the time Juana
had been trying to rescue something of the old peace, of
the time before the pearl. But now it was gone, and there
was no retrieving it. And knowing this, she abandoned
the past instantly. There was nothing to do but to save
themselves.

Her pain was gone now, her slowness. Quickly she dragged the dead man from the pathway into the shelter of the brush. She went to Kino and sponged his face with her wet skirt. His senses were coming back and he moaned.

"They have taken the pearl. I have lost it. Now it is over," he said. "The pearl is gone."

Juana quieted him as she would quiet a sick child. "Hush," she said. "Here is your pearl. I found it in the path. Can you hear me now? Here is your pearl. Can you understand? You have killed a man. We must go away. They will come for us, can you understand? We must be gone before the daylight comes."

"I was attacked," Kino said uneasily. "I struck to save my life."

"Do you remember yesterday?" Juana asked. "Do you think that will matter? Do you remember the men of the city? Do you think your explanation will help?"

Kino drew a great breath and fought off his weakness. "No," he said. "You are right." And his will hardened and he was a man again.

"Go to our house and bring Coyotito," he said, "and bring all the corn we have. I will drag the canoe into the water and we will go."

He took his knife and left her. He stumbled toward the beach and he came to his canoe. And when the light broke through again he saw that a great hole had been knocked in the bottom. And a searing rage came to him and gave him strength. Now the darkness was closing in on his family; now the evil music filled the night, hung over the mangroves, skirled in the wave beat. The canoe of his grandfather, plastered over and over, and a splintered hole broken in it. This was an evil beyond thinking. The killing of a man was not so evil as the killing of a boat. For a boat does not have sons, and a boat cannot protect itself, and a wounded boat does not heal. There was sorrow in Kino's rage, but this last thing had tightened him beyond breaking. He was an animal now, for hiding, for attacking, and he lived only to preserve himself and his family. He was not conscious of the pain in his head. He leaped up the beach, through the brush line toward his brush house, and it did not occur to him to take one of the canoes of his neighbors. Never once did the thought enter his head, any more than he could have conceived breaking a boat.

The roosters were crowing and the dawn was not far off. Smoke of the first fires seeped out through the walls of the brush houses, and the first smell of cooking corncakes was in the air. Already the dawn birds were scampering in the bushes. The weak moon was losing its light and the clouds thickened and curdled to the southward. The wind blew freshly into the estuary, a nervous, restless wind with the smell of storm on its breath, and there was change and uneasiness in the air.

Kino, hurrying toward his house, felt a surge of exhilaration. Now he was not confused, for there was only one thing to do, and Kino's hand went first to the great pearl in his shirt and then to his knife hanging under his shirt.

He saw a little glow ahead of him, and then without interval a tall flame leaped up in the dark with a crackling roar, and a tall edifice of fire lighted the pathway. Kino broke into a run; it was his brush house, he knew. And he knew that these houses could burn down in a very few moments. And as he ran a scuttling figure ran toward him—Juana, with Coyotito in her arms and Kino's shoulder blanket clutched in her hand. The baby moaned with fright, and Juana's eyes were wide and terrified. Kino could see the house was gone, and he did not question Juana. He knew, but she said, "It was torn up and the floor dug—even the baby's box turned out, and as I looked they put the fire to the outside."

The fierce light of the burning house lighted Kino's face strongly. "Who?" he demanded.

"I don't know," she said. "The dark ones."

The neighbors were tumbling from their houses now, and they watched the falling sparks and stamped them out to save their own houses. Suddenly Kino was afraid. The light made him afraid. He remembered the man lying dead in the brush beside the path, and he took Juana by the arm and drew her into the shadow of a house away from the light, for light was danger to him. For a moment he considered and then he worked among the shadows until he came to the house of Juan Tomás, his brother, and he slipped into the doorway and drew Juana after him. Outside, he could hear the squeal of children and the shouts of the neighbors, for his friends thought he might be inside the burning house.

The house of Juan Tomás was almost exactly like Kino's house; nearly all the brush houses were alike, and all leaked light and air, so that Juana and Kino, sitting in the corner of the brother's house, could see the leaping flames through the wall. They saw the flames tall and furious, they saw the roof fall and watched the fire die down as quickly as a twig fire dies. They heard the cries of warning of their friends, and the shrill, keening cry of Apolonia, wife of Juan Tomás. She, being the nearest woman relative, raised a formal lament for the dead of the family.

Apolonia realized that she was wearing her second-best

head shawl and she rushed to her house to get her fine new one. As she rummaged in a box by the wall, Kino's voice said quietly, "Apolonia, do not cry out. We are not hurt."

"How do you come here?" she demanded.

"Do not question," he said. "Go now to Juan Tomás and bring him here and tell no one else. This is important to us, Apolonia."

She paused, her hands helpless in front of her, and then, "Yes, my brother-in-law," she said.

In a few moments Juan Tomás came back with her. He lighted a candle and came to them where they crouched in a corner and he said, "Apolonia, see to the door, and do not let anyone enter." He was older, Juan Tomás, and he assumed the authority. "Now, my brother," he said.

"I was attacked in the dark," said Kino. "And in the fight I have killed a man."

"Who?" asked Juan Tomás quickly.

"I do not know. It is all darkness—all darkness and shape of darkness."

"It is the pearl," said Juan Tomás. "There is a devil in this pearl. You should have sold it and passed on the devil. Perhaps you can still sell it and buy peace for yourself."

And Kino said, "Oh, my brother, an insult has been put on me that is deeper than my life. For on the beach my canoe is broken, my house is burned, and in the brush a dead man lies. Every escape is cut off. You must hide us, my brother."

And Kino, looking closely, saw deep worry come into his brother's eyes and he forestalled him in a possible refusal. "Not for long," he said quickly. "Only until a day has passed and the new night has come. Then we will go."

"I will hide you," said Juan Tomás.

"I do not want to bring danger to you," Kino said. "I know I am like a leprosy. I will go tonight and then you will be safe."

"I will protect you," said Juan Tomás, and he called, "Apolonia, close up the door. Do not even whisper that Kino is here."

They sat silently all day in the darkness of the house, and they could hear the neighbors speaking of them. Through the walls of the house they could watch their neighbors raking through the ashes to find the bones. Crouching in the house of Juan Tomás, they heard the shock go into their neighbors' minds at the news of the broken boat. Juan Tomás went out among the neighbors to divert their suspicions, and he gave them theories and ideas of what had happened to Kino and to Juana and to the baby. To one he said, "I think they have gone south along the coast to escape the evil that was on them." And to another, "Kino would never leave the sea. Perhaps he found another boat." And he said, "Apolonia is ill with grief."

And in that day the wind rose up to beat the Gulf and tore the kelps and weeds that lined the shore, and the wind cried through the brush houses and no boat was safe on the water. Then Juan Tomás told among the neighbors, "Kino is gone. If he went to the sea, he is drowned by now." And after each trip among the neighbors Juan Tomás came back with something borrowed. He brought a little woven straw bag of red beans and a gourd full of rice. He borrowed a cup of dried peppers and a block of salt, and he brought in a long working knife, eighteen inches long and heavy, as a small ax, a tool and a weapon. And when Kino saw this knife his eyes lighted up, and he fondled the blade and his thumb tested the edge.

The wind screamed over the Gulf and turned the water white, and the mangroves plunged like frightened cattle, and a fine sandy dust arose from the land and hung in a stifling cloud over the sea. The wind drove off the clouds and skimmed the sky clean and drifted the sand of the country like snow.

Then Juan Tomás, when the evening approached, talked long with his brother. "Where will you go?"

"To the north," said Kino. "I have heard that there are cities in the north."

"Avoid the shore," said Juan Tomás. "They are making a party to search the shore. The men in the city will look for you. Do you still have the pearl?"

"I have it," said Kino. "And I will keep it. I might have given it as a gift, but now it is my misfortune and my life and I will keep it." His eyes were hard and cruel and bitter.

Coyotito whimpered and Juana muttered little magics over him to make him silent.

"The wind is good," said Juan Tomás. "There will be no tracks."

They left quietly in the dark before the moon had risen. The family stood formally in the house of Juan Tomás. Juana carried Coyotito on her back, covered and held in by her head shawl, and the baby slept, cheek turned sideways against her shoulder. The head shawl covered the baby, and one end of it came across Juana's nose to protect her from the evil night air. Juan Tomás embraced his brother with the double embrace and kissed him on both cheeks. "Go with God," he said, and it was like a death. "You will not give up the pearl?"

"This pearl has become my soul," said Kino. "If I give it up I shall lose my soul. Go thou also with God."

6

The wind blew fierce and strong, and it pelted them with bits of sticks, sand, and little rocks. Juana and Kino gathered their clothing tighter about them and covered their noses and went out into the world. The sky was brushed clean by the wind and the stars were cold in a black sky. The two walked carefully, and they avoided the center of the town where some sleeper in a doorway might see them pass. For the town closed itself in against the night, and anyone who moved about in the darkness would be noticeable. Kino threaded his way around the edge of the city and turned north, north by the stars, and found the rutted sandy road that led through the brushy country toward Loreto where the miraculous Virgin has her station.

Kino could feel the blown sand against his ankles and he was glad, for he knew there would be no tracks. The little light from the stars made out for him the narrow road through the brushy country. And Kino could hear the pad of Juana's feet behind him. He went quickly and quietly, and Juana trotted behind him to keep up.

Some ancient thing stirred in Kino. Through his fear of dark and the devils that haunt the night, there came a rush of exhilaration; some animal thing was moving in him so that he was cautious and wary and dangerous; some ancient thing out of the past of his people was alive in him. The wind was at his back and the stars guided him. The wind cried and whisked in the brush, and the family went on monotonously, hour after hour. They passed no one and saw no one. At last, to their right, the waning moon arose, and when it came up the wind died down, and the land was still.

Now they could see the little road ahead of them, deep cut with sand-drifted wheel tracks. With the wind gone there would be footprints, but they were a good distance from the town and perhaps their tracks might not be noticed. Kino walked carefully in a wheel rut, and Juana followed in his path. One big cart, going to the town in the morning, could wipe out every trace of their passage.

All night they walked and never changed their pace. Once Coyotito awakened, and Juana shifted him in front of her and soothed him until he went to sleep again. And the evils of the night were about them. The coyotes cried and laughed in the brush, and the owls screeched and hissed over their heads. And once some large animal lumbered away, crackling the undergrowth as it went. And Kino gripped the handle of the big working knife and took a sense of protection from it.

The music of the pearl was triumphant in Kino's head, and the quiet melody of the family underlay it, and they wove themselves into the soft padding of sandaled feet in the dust. All night they walked, and in the first dawn Kino searched the roadside for a covert to lie in during the day. He found his place near to the road, a little clearing where deer might have lain, and it was curtained thickly with the dry brittle trees that lined the road. And when Juana had seated herself and had settled to nurse the baby, Kino went back to the road. He broke a branch and carefully swept the footprints where they had turned from the roadway. And then, in the first light, he heard the creak of a wagon, and he crouched beside the road and watched a heavy two-wheeled cart go by, drawn by slouching oxen. And when it had passed out of sight, he went back to the roadway and looked at the rut and found that the footprints were gone. And again he swept out his traces and went back to Juana.

She gave him the soft corncakes Apolonia had packed for them, and after a while she slept a little. But Kino sat on the ground and stared at the earth in front of him. He watched the ants moving, a little column of them near to his foot, and he put his foot in their path. Then the column climbed over his instep and continued on its way, and Kino left his foot there and watched them move over it.

The sun arose hotly. They were not near the Gulf now, and the air was dry and hot so that the brush cricked with heat and a good resinous smell came from it. And when Juana awakened, when the sun was high, Kino told her things she knew already.

"Beware of that kind of tree there," he said, pointing. "Do not touch it, for if you do and then touch your eyes, it will blind you. And beware of the tree that bleeds. See, that one over there. For if you break it the red blood will flow from it, and it is evil luck." And she nodded and smiled a little at him, for she knew these things.

"Will they follow us?" she asked. "Do you think they will try to find us?"

"They will try," said Kino. "Whoever finds us will take the pearl. Oh, they will try."

And Juana said, "Perhaps the dealers were right and the

pearl has no value. Perhaps this has all been an illusion."

Kino reached into his clothes and brought out the pearl. He let the sun play on it until it burned in his eyes. "No," he said, "they would not have tried to steal it if it had been valueless."

"Do you know who attacked you? Was it the dealers?"

"I do not know," he said. "I didn't see them."

He looked into his pearl to find his vision. "When we sell it at last, I will have a rifle," he said, and he looked into the shining surface for his rifle, but he saw only a huddled dark body on the ground with shining blood dripping from its throat. And he said quickly, "We will be married in a great church." And in the pearl he saw Juana with her beaten face crawling home through the night. "Our son must learn to read," he said frantically. And there in the pearl Coyotito's face, thick and feverish from the medicine.

And Kino thrust the pearl back into his clothing, and the music of the pearl had become sinister in his ears, and it was interwoven with the music of evil.

The hot sun beat on the earth so that Kino and Juana moved into the lacy shade of the brush, and small gray birds scampered on the ground in the shade. In the heat of the day Kino relaxed and covered his eyes with his hat and wrapped his blanket about his face to keep the flies off, and he slept.

But Juana did not sleep. She sat quiet as a stone and her face was quiet. Her mouth was still swollen where Kino had struck her, and big flies buzzed around the cut on her chin. But she sat as still as a sentinel, and when Coyotito awakened she placed him on the ground in front of her and watched him wave his arms and kick his feet, and he smiled and gurgled at her until she smiled too. She picked up a little twig from the ground and tickled him, and she gave him water from the gourd she carried in her bundle.

Kino stirred in a dream, and he cried out in a guttural voice, and his hand moved in symbolic fighting. And then he moaned and sat up suddenly, his eyes wide and his nostrils flaring. He listened and heard only the cricking heat and the hiss of distance.

"What is it?" Juana asked.

"Hush," he said.

"You were dreaming."

"Perhaps." But he was restless, and when she gave him a corncake from her store he paused in his chewing to listen. He was uneasy and nervous; he glanced over his shoulder; he lifted the big knife and felt its edge. When Coyotito gurgled on the ground Kino said, "Keep him quiet."

"What is the matter?" Juana asked.

"I don't know."

He listened again, an animal light in his eyes. He stood up then, silently; and crouched low, he threaded his way through the brush toward the road. But he did not step into the road; he crept into the cover of a thorny tree and peered out along the way he had come.

And then he saw them moving along. His body stiffened and he drew down his head and peeked out from under a fallen branch. In the distance he could see three figures, two on foot and one on horseback. But he knew what they were, and a chill of fear went through him. Even in the distance he could see the two on foot moving slowly along, bent low to the ground. Here, one would pause and look at the earth, while the other joined him. They were the trackers, they could follow the trail of a bighorn sheep in the stone mountains. They were as sensitive as hounds. Here, he and Juana might have stepped out of the wheel rut, and these people from the inland, these hunters, could follow, could read a broken straw or a little tumbled pile of dust. Behind them, on a horse, was a dark man, his nose covered with a blanket, and across his saddle a rifle gleamed in the sun.

Kino lay as rigid as the tree limb. He barely breathed, and his eyes went to the place where he had swept out the track. Even the sweeping might be a message to the trackers. He knew these inland hunters. In a country where there was little game they managed to live because of their ability to hunt, and they were hunting him. They scuttled over the ground like animals and found a sign and crouched over it while the horseman waited.

The trackers whined a little, like excited dogs on a warming trail. Kino slowly drew his big knife to his hand and made it ready. He knew what he must do. If the trackers found the swept place, he must leap for the horseman, kill him quickly and take the rifle. That was his only chance in the world. And as the three drew nearer on the road, Kino dug little pits with his sandaled toes so that he could leap without warning, so that his feet would not slip. He had only a little vision under the fallen limb.

Now Juana, back in her hidden place, heard the pad of the horse's hoofs, and Coyotito gurgled. She took him up quickly and put him under her shawl and gave him her breast and he was silent.

When the trackers came near, Kino could see only their legs and only the legs of the horse from under the fallen branch. He saw the dark horny feet of the men and their ragged white clothes, and he heard the creak of leather of the saddle and the clink of spurs. The trackers stopped at the swept place and studied it, and the horseman stopped. The horse flung his head up against the bit and the bit-roller clicked under his tongue and the horse snorted. Then the dark trackers turned and studied the horse and watched his ears.

Kino was not breathing, but his back arched a little and the muscles of his arms and legs stood out with tension and a line of sweat formed on his upper lip. For a long moment the trackers bent over the road, and then they moved on slowly, studying the ground ahead of them, and the horseman moved after them. The trackers scuttled along, stopping, looking, and hurrying on. They would be back, Kino knew. They would be circling and searching, peeping, stooping, and they would come back sooner or later to his covered track.

He slid backward and did not bother to cover his tracks. He could not; too many little signs were there, too many broken twigs and scuffed places and displaced stones. And there was a panic in Kino now, a panic of flight. The trackers would find his trail, he knew it. There was no escape, except in flight. He edged away from the road and went quickly and silently to the hidden place where Juana was. She looked up at him in question.

"Trackers," he said. "Come!"

And then a helplessness and a hopelessness swept over him, and his face went black and his eyes were sad. "Perhaps I should let them take me."

Instantly Juana was on her feet and her hand lay on his arm. "You have the pearl," she cried hoarsely. "Do you think they would take you back alive to say they had stolen it?"

His hand strayed limply to the place where the pearl was hidden under his clothes. "They will find it," he said weakly.

"Come," she said. "Come!"

And when he did not respond, "Do you think they would let me live? Do you think they would let the little one here live?"

Her goading struck into his brain; his lips snarled and his eyes were fierce again. "Come," he said. "We will go into the mountains. Maybe we can lose them in the mountains."

Frantically he gathered the gourds and the little bags that were their property. Kino carried a bundle in his left hand, but the big knife swung free in his right hand. He parted the brush for Juana and they hurried to the west, toward the high stone mountains. They trotted quickly through the tangle of the undergrowth. This was panic flight. Kino did not try to conceal his passage as he trotted, kicking the stones, knocking the telltale leaves from the little trees. The high sun streamed down on the dry creaking earth so that even the vegetation ticked in protest. But ahead were the naked granite mountains, rising out of erosion rubble and standing monolithic against the sky. And Kino ran for the high place, as nearly all animals do when they are pursued.

This land was waterless, furred with the cacti which could store water and with the great-rooted brush which could reach deep into the earth for a little moisture and get along on very little. And underfoot was not soil but broken rock, split into small cubes, great slabs, but none of it water-rounded. Little tufts of sad dry grass grew between the stones, grass that had sprouted with one single rain and headed, dropped its seed, and died. Horned toads watched the family go by and turned their little pivoting dragon heads. And now and then a great jackrabbit, disturbed in his shade, bumped away and hid behind the nearest rock. The singing heat lay over this desert country, and ahead the stone mountains looked cool and welcoming.

And Kino fled. He knew what would happen. A little way along the road the trackers would become aware that they had missed the path, and they would come back, searching and judging, and in a little while they would find the place where Kino and Juana had rested. From there it would be easy for them—these little stones, the fallen leaves and the whipped branches, the scuffed places where a foot had slipped. Kino could see them in his mind, slipping along the track, whining a little with eagerness, and behind them, dark and half disinterested, the horseman with the rifle. His work would come last, for he would not take them back. Oh, the music of evil sang loud in Kino's head now, it sang with the whine of heat and with the dry ringing of snake rattles. It was not large and overwhelming now, but secret and poisonous, and the pounding of his heart gave it undertone and rhythm.

The way began to rise, and as it did the rocks grew larger. But now Kino had put a little distance between his family and the trackers. Now, on the first rise, he rested. He climbed a great boulder and looked back over the shimmering country, but he could not see his enemies, not even the tall horseman riding through the brush. Juana had squatted in the shade of the boulder. She raised her bottle of water to Coyotito's lips; his little dried tongue sucked greedily at it. She looked up at Kino when he came back; she saw him examine her ankles, cut and scratched from the stones and brush, and she covered them quickly with her skirt. Then she handed the bottle to him, but he shook his head. Her eyes were bright in her tired face. Kino moistened his cracked lips with his tongue.

"Juana," he said, "I will go on and you will hide. I will lead them into the mountains, and when they have gone past, you will go north to Loreto or to Santa Rosalia. Then, if I can escape them, I will come to you. It is the only safe way."

She looked full into his eyes for a moment. "No," she said. "We go with you."

"I can go faster alone," he said harshly. "You will put the little one in more danger if you go with me."

"No," said Juana.

"You must. It is the wise thing and it is my wish," he said.

"No," said Juana.

He looked then for weakness in her face, for fear or irresolution, and there was none. Her eyes were very bright. He shrugged his shoulders helplessly then, but he had taken strength from her. When they moved on it was no longer panic flight.

The country, as it rose toward the mountains, changed rapidly. Now there were long outcroppings of granite with deep crevices between, and Kino walked on bare unmarkable stone when he could and leaped from ledge to ledge. He knew that wherever the trackers lost his path they must circle and lose time before they found it again. And so he did not go straight for the mountains any more; he moved in zig-zags, and sometimes he cut back to the south and left a sign and then went toward the mountains over bare stone again. And the path rose steeply now, so that he panted a little as he went.

The sun moved downward toward the bare stone teeth of the mountains, and Kino set his direction for a dark and shadowy cleft in the range. If there were any water at all, it would be there where he could see, even in the distance, a hint of foliage. And if there were any passage through the smooth stone range, it would be by this same deep cleft. It had its danger, for the trackers would think of it too, but the empty water bottle did not let that consideration enter. And as the sun lowered, Kino and Juana struggled wearily up the steep slope toward the cleft.

High in the gray stone mountains, under a frowning peak, a little spring bubbled out of a rupture in the stone. It was fed by shade-preserved snow in the summer, and now and then it died completely and bare rocks and dry algae were on its bottom. But nearly always it gushed out, cold and clean and lovely. In the times when the quick rains fell, it might become a freshet and send its column of white water crashing down the mountain cleft, but nearly always it was a lean little spring. It bubbled out into a pool and then fell a hundred feet to another pool, and this one, overflowing, dropped again, so that it continued, down and down, until it came to the rubble of the upland, and there it disappeared altogether. There wasn't much left of it then anyway, for every time it fell over an escarpment the thirsty air drank it, and it splashed from the pools to the dry vegetation. The animals from miles around came to drink from the little pools, and the wild sheep and the deer, the pumas and raccoons, and the mice—all came to drink. And the birds which spent the day in the brushland came at night to the little pools that were like steps in the mountain cleft. Beside this tiny stream, wherever enough earth collected for root-hold, colonies of plants grew, wild grape and little palms, maidenhair fern, hibiscus, and tall pampas grass with feathery rods raised above the spike leaves. And in the pool lived frogs and waterskaters, and waterworms crawled on the bottom of the pool. Everything that loved water came to these few shallow places. The cats took their prey there, and strewed feathers and lapped water through their bloody teeth. The little pools were places of life because of the water, and places of killing because of the water, too.

The lowest step, where the stream collected before it tumbled down a hundred feet and disappeared into the rubbly desert, was a little platform of stone and sand. Only a pencil of water fell into the pool, but it was enough to keep the pool full and to keep the ferns green in the underhang of the cliff, and wild grape climbed the stone mountain and all manner of little plants found comfort here. The freshets had made a small sandy beach through which the pool flowed, and bright green watercress grew in the damp sand. The beach was cut and scarred and padded by the feet of animals that had come to drink and to hunt.

The sun had passed over the stone mountains when Kino and Juana struggled up the steep broken slope and came at last to the water. From this step they could look out over the sunbeaten desert to the blue Gulf in the distance. They came utterly weary to the pool, and Juana slumped to her knees and first washed Coyotito's face and then filled her bottle and gave him a drink. And the baby was weary and petulant, and he cried softly until Juana gave him her breast, and then he gurgled and clucked against her. Kino drank long and thirstily at the pool. For a moment, then, he stretched out beside the water and relaxed all his muscles and watched Juana feeding the baby, and then he got to his feet and went to the edge of the step where the water slipped over, and he searched the distance carefully. His eyes set on a point and he became rigid. Far down the slope he could see the two trackers; they were little more than dots or scurrying ants and behind them a larger ant.

Juana had turned to look at him and she saw his back stiffen.

"How far?" she asked quietly.

"They will be here by evening," said Kino. He looked up the long steep chimney of the cleft where the water came down. "We must go west," he said, and his eyes searched the stone shoulder behind the cleft. And thirty feet up on the gray shoulder he saw a series of little erosion caves. He slipped off his sandals and clambered up to them, gripping the bare stone with his toes, and he looked into the shallow caves. They were only a few feet deep, wind-hollowed scoops, but they sloped slightly downward and back. Kino crawled into the largest one and lay down and knew that he could not be seen from the outside. Quickly he went back to Juana.

"You must go up there. Perhaps they will not find us there," he said.

Without question she filled her water bottle to the top, and then Kino helped her up to the shallow cave and brought up the packages of food and passed them to her. And Juana sat in the cave entrance and watched him. She saw that he did not try to erase their tracks in the sand. Instead, he climbed up the brush cliff beside the water, clawing and tearing at the ferns and wild grape as he went. And when he had climbed a hundred feet to the next bench, he came down again. He looked carefully at the smooth rock shoulder toward the cave to see that there was no trace of passage, and last he climbed up and crept into the cave beside Juana.

"When they go up," he said, "we will slip away, down to the lowlands again. I am afraid only that the baby may cry. You must see that he does not cry."

"He will not cry," she said, and she raised the baby's face to her own and looked into his eyes and he stared solemnly back at her.

"He knows," said Juana.

Now Kino lay in the cave entrance, his chin braced on his crossed arms, and he watched the blue shadow of the mountain move out across the brushy desert below until it reached the Gulf, and the long twilight of the shadow was over the land.

The trackers were long in coming, as though they had trouble with the trail Kino had left. It was dusk when they came at last to the little pool. And all three were on foot now, for a horse could not climb the last steep slope. From above they were thin figures in the evening. The two trackers scurried about on the little beach, and they saw Kino's progress up the cliff before they drank. The man with the rifle sat down and rested himself, and the trackers squatted near him, and in the evening the points of their cigarettes glowed and receded. And then Kino could see that they were eating, and the soft murmur of their voices came to him.

Then darkness fell, deep and black in the mountain cleft. The animals that used the pool came near and smelled men there and drifted away again into the darkness.

He heard a murmur behind him. Juana was whispering, "Coyotito." She was begging him to be quiet. Kino heard the baby whimper, and he knew from the muffled sounds that Juana had covered his head with her shawl.

Down on the beach a match flared, and in its momentary

light Kino saw that two of the men were sleeping, curled up like dogs, while the third watched, and he saw the glint of the rifle in the match light. And then the match died, but it left a picture on Kino's eyes. He could see it, just how each man was, two sleeping curled up and the third squatting in the sand with the rifle between his knees.

Kino moved silently back into the cave. Juana's eyes were two sparks reflecting a low star. Kino crawled quietly close to her and he put his lips near to her cheek.

"There is a way," he said.

"But they will kill you."

"If I get first to the one with the rifle," Kino said, "I must get to him first, then I will be all right. Two are sleeping."

Her hand crept out from under her shawl and gripped his arm. "They will see your white clothes in the starlight."

"No," he said. "And I must go before moonrise."

He searched for a soft word and then gave it up. "If they kill me," he said, "lie quietly. And when they are gone away, go to Loreto."

Her hand shook a little, holding his wrist.

"There is no choice," he said. "It is the only way. They will find us in the morning."

Her voice trembled a little. "Go with God," she said.

He peered closely at her and he could see her large eyes. His hand fumbled out and found the baby, and for a moment his palm lay on Coyotito's head. And then Kino raised his hand and touched Juana's cheek, and she held her breath.

Against the sky in the cave entrance Juana could see that Kino was taking off his white clothes, for dirty and ragged though they were they would show up against the dark night. His own brown skin was a better protection for him.

And then she saw how he hooked his amulet neck-string about the horn handle of his great knife, so that it hung down in front of him and left both hands free. He did not come back to her. For a moment his body was black in the cave entrance, crouched and silent, and then he was gone.

Juana moved to the entrance and looked out. She peered like an owl from the hole in the mountain, and the baby slept under the blanket on her back, his face turned sideways against her neck and shoulder. She could feel his warm breath against her skin, and Juana whispered her combination of prayer and magic, her Hail Marys and her ancient intercession, against the black unhuman things.

The night seemed a little less dark when she looked out, and to the east there was a lightning in the sky, down near the horizon where the moon would show. And, looking down, she could see the cigarette of the man on watch.

Kino edged like a slow lizard down the smooth rock shoulder. He had turned his neck-string so that the great knife hung down from his back and could not clash against the stone. His spread fingers gripped the mountain, and his bare toes found support through contact, and even his chest lay against the stone so that he would not slip. For any sound, a rolling pebble or a sigh, a little slip of flesh on rock, would rouse the watchers below. Any sound that was not germane to the night would make them alert. But the night was not silent; the little tree frogs that lived near the stream twittered like birds, and the high metallic ringing of the cicadas filled the mountain cleft. And Kino's own music was in his head, the music of the enemy, low and pulsing, nearly asleep. But the Song of the Family had become as fierce and sharp and feline as the snarl of a female puma. The family song was alive now and driving him down on the dark enemy. The harsh cicada seemed to take up its melody, and the twittering tree frogs called little phrases of it.

And Kino crept silently as a shadow down the smooth mountain face. One bare foot moved a few inches and the toes touched the stone and gripped, and the other foot a few inches, and then the palm of one hand a little downward, and then the other hand, until the whole body, without seeming to move, had moved. Kino's mouth was open so that even his breath would make no sound, for he knew that he was not invisible. If the watcher, sensing movement, looked at the dark place against the stone which was his body, he could see him. Kino must move so slowly he would not draw the watcher's eyes. It took him a long time to reach the bottom and to crouch behind a little dwarf palm. His heart thundered in his chest and his hands and face were wet with sweat. He crouched and took great slow long breaths to calm himself.

Only twenty feet separated him from the enemy now, and he tried to remember the ground between. Was there any stone which might trip him in his rush? He kneaded his legs against cramp and found that his muscles were jerking after their long tension. And then he looked apprehensively to the east. The moon would rise in a few moments now, and he must attack before it rose. He could see the outline of the watcher, but the sleeping men were below his vision. It was the watcher Kino must find—must find quickly and without hesitation. Silently he drew the amulet string over his shoulder and loosened the loop from the horn handle of his great knife.

He was too late, for as he rose from his crouch the silver edge of the moon slipped above the eastern horizon, and Kino sank back behind his bush.

The Pearl

It was an old and ragged moon, but it threw hard light and hard shadow into the mountain cleft, and now Kino could see the seated figure of the watcher on the little beach beside the pool. The watcher gazed full at the moon, and then he lighted another cigarette, and the match illumined his dark face for a moment. There could be no waiting now; when the watcher turned his head, Kino must leap. His legs were as tight as wound springs.

And then from above came a little murmuring cry. The watcher turned his head to listen and then he stood up, and one of the sleepers stirred on the ground and awakened and asked quietly, "What is it?"

"I don't know," said the watcher. "It sounded like a cry, almost like a human—like a baby."

The man who had been sleeping said, "You can't tell. Some coyote bitch with a litter. I've heard a coyote pup cry like a baby."

The sweat rolled in drops down Kino's forehead and fell into his eyes and burned them. The little cry came again and the watcher looked up the side of the hill to the dark cave.

"Coyote maybe," he said, and Kino heard the harsh click as he cocked the rifle.

"If it's a coyote, this will stop it," the watcher said as he raised the gun.

Kino was in mid-leap when the gun crashed and the barrel-flash made a picture on his eyes. The great knife swung and crunched hollowly. It bit through neck and deep into chest, and Kino was a terrible machine now. He grasped the rifle even as he wrenched free his knife. His strength and his movement and his speed were a machine. He whirled and struck the head of the seated man like a

86

melon. The third man scrabbled away like a crab, slipped into the pool, and then he began to climb frantically, to climb up the cliff where the water penciled down. His hands and feet threshed in the tangle of the wild grapevine, and he whimpered and gibbered as he tried to get up. But Kino had become as cold and deadly as steel. Deliberately he threw the lever of the rifle, and then he raised the gun and aimed deliberately and fired. He saw his enemy tumble backward into the pool, and Kino strode to the water. In the moonlight he could see the frantic frightened eyes, and Kino aimed and fired between the eyes.

And then Kino stood uncertainly. Something was wrong, some signal was trying to get through to his brain. Tree frogs and cicadas were silent now. And then Kino's brain cleared from its red concentration and he knew the sound—the keening, moaning, rising hysterical cry from the little cave in the side of the stone mountain, the cry of death.

Everyone in La Paz remembers the return of the family; there may be some old ones who saw it, but those whose fathers and whose grandfathers told it to them remember it nevertheless. It is an event that happened to everyone.

It was late in the golden afternoon when the first little boys ran hysterically in the town and spread the word that Kino and Juana were coming back. And everyone hurried to see them. The sun was settling toward the western mountains and the shadows on the ground were long. And perhaps that was what left the deep impression on those who saw them.

The two came from the rutted country road into the city, and they were not walking in single file, Kino ahead and

Juana behind, as usual, but side by side. The sun was behind them and their long shadows stalked ahead, and they seemed to carry two towers of darkness with them. Kino had a rifle across his arm and Juana carried her shawl like a sack over her shoulder. And in it was a small limp heavy bundle. The shawl was crusted with dried blood, and the bundle swayed a little as she walked. Her face was hard and lined and leathery with fatigue and with the tightness with which she fought fatigue. And her wide eyes stared inward on herself. She was as remote and as removed as Heaven. Kino's lips were thin and his jaws tight, and the people say that he carried fear with him, that he was as dangerous as a rising storm. The people say that the two seemed to be removed from human experience; that they had gone through pain and had come out on the other side; that there was almost a magical protection about them. And those people who had rushed to see them crowded back and let them pass and did not speak to them.

Kino and Juana walked through the city as though it were not there. Their eyes glanced neither right nor left nor up nor down, but stared only straight ahead. Their legs moved a little jerkily, like well-made wooden dolls, and they carried pillars of black fear about them. And as they walked through the stone and plaster city brokers peered at them from barred windows and servants put one eye to a slitted gate and mothers turned the faces of their youngest children inward against their skirts. Kino and Juana strode side by side through the stone and plaster city and down among the brush houses, and the neighbors stood back and let them pass. Juan Tomás raised his hand in greeting and did not say the greeting and left his hand in the air for a moment uncertainly.

In Kino's ears the Song of the Family was as fierce as a cry. He was immune and terrible, and his song had become a battle cry. They trudged past the burned square where their house had been without even looking at it. They cleared the brush that edged the beach and picked their way down the shore toward the water. And they did not look toward Kino's broken canoe.

And when they came to the water's edge they stopped and stared out over the Gulf. And then Kino laid the rifle down, and he dug among his clothes, and then he held the great pearl in his hand. He looked into its surface and it was gray and ulcerous. Evil faces peered from it into his eyes, and he saw the light of burning. And in the surface of the pearl he saw the frantic eyes of the man in the pool. And in the surface of the pearl he saw Coyotito lying in the little cave with the top of his head shot away. And the pearl was ugly; it was gray, like a malignant growth. And Kino heard the music of the pearl, distorted and insane. Kino's hand shook a little, and he turned slowly to Juana and held the pearl out to her. She stood beside him, still holding her dead bundle over her shoulder. She looked at the pearl in his hand for a moment and then she looked into Kino's eyes and said softly, "No, you."

And Kino drew back his arm and flung the pearl with all his might. Kino and Juana watched it go, winking and glimmering under the setting sun. They saw the little splash in the distance, and they stood side by side watching the place for a long time.

And the pearl settled into the lovely green water and dropped toward the bottom. The waving branches of the algae called to it and beckoned to it. The lights on its surface were green and lovely. It settled down to the sand bottom

among the fern-like plants. Above, the surface of the water was a green mirror. And the pearl lay on the floor of the sea. A crab scampering over the bottom raised a little cloud of sand, and when it settled the pearl was gone.

And the music of the pearl drifted to a whisper and disappeared.

PENGUIN CLASSICS

www.penguinclassics.com

- Details about every Penguin Classic

- Advanced information about forthcoming titles

- Hundreds of author biographies

- FREE resources including critical essays on the books and their historical background, reader's and teacher's guides.

- Links to other web resources for the Classics

- Discussion area

- Online review copy ordering for academics

- Competitions with prizes, and challenging Classics trivia quizzes

PENGUIN CLASSICS ONLINE

READ MORE IN PENGUIN

In every corner of the world, on every subject under the sun, Penguin represents quality and variety – the very best in publishing today.

For complete information about books available from Penguin – including Puffins, Penguin Classics and Arkana – and how to order them, write to us at the appropriate address below. Please note that for copyright reasons the selection of books varies from country to country.

In the United Kingdom: Please write to *Dept. EP, Penguin Books Ltd, Bath Road, Harmondsworth, West Drayton, Middlesex UB7 0DA*

In the United States: Please write to *Consumer Services, Penguin Putnam Inc., 405 Murray Hill Parkway, East Rutherford, New Jersey 07073-2136.* VISA and MasterCard holders call 1-800-631-8571 to order Penguin titles

In Canada: Please write to *Penguin Books Canada Ltd, 10 Alcorn Avenue Suite 300, Toronto, Ontario M4V 3B2*

In Australia: Please write to *Penguin Books Australia Ltd, 487 Maroondah Highway, Ringwood, Victoria 3134*

In New Zealand: Please write to *Penguin Books (NZ) Ltd, Private Bag 102902, North Shore Mail Centre, Auckland 10*

In India: Please write to *Penguin Books India Pvt Ltd, 11 Community Centre, Panchsheel Park, New Delhi 110017*

In the Netherlands: Please write to *Penguin Books Netherlands bv, Postbus 3507, NL-1001 AH Amsterdam*

In Germany: Please write to *Penguin Books Deutschland GmbH, Metzlerstrasse 26, 60594 Frankfurt am Main*

In Spain: Please write to *Penguin Books S. A., Bravo Murillo 19, 1°B, 28015 Madrid*

In Italy: Please write to *Penguin Italia s.r.l., Via Vittorio Emanuele 45/a, 20094 Corsico, Milano*

In France: Please write to *Penguin France, 12, Rue Prosper Ferradou, 31700 Blagnac*

In Japan: Please write to *Penguin Books Japan Ltd, Iidabashi KM-Bldg, 2-23-9 Koraku, Bunkyo-Ku, Tokyo 112-0004*

In South Africa: Please write to *Penguin Books South Africa (Pty) Ltd, P.O. Box 751093, Gardenview, 2047 Johannesburg*

BY THE SAME AUTHOR

The Red Pony

Like most ten-year-old boys, Jody Tiflin has the urge for rebellion as well as the need to be loved. In these stories, Jody begins to learn about adulthood – its pains, its responsibilities and its problems – through his acceptance of his father's gifts. First he is given a red pony and later he is promised the colt of a bay mare. Yet both of these gifts bring tragedy as well as joy, and Jody is taught not only the harsh lessons of life and death, but made painfully aware of the fallibility of adults.

Cannery Row

In the din and stink that is Cannery Row a colourful blend of misfits survive side by side in a jumble of adventure and mischief. Lee Chong, the astute owner of the fantastically well-stocked grocery store, is also the proprietor of the Palace Flophouse that Mack and his troupe of good-natured 'boys' call home. Dora, of the flaming orange hair and taste for Nile-green dresses, runs the brothel with clockwork efficiency. Doc, who owns the laboratory, is the fount of all generosity and wisdom. Everybody wants to do something nice for Doc: the trouble is, he always ends up paying. Packed with invention and *joie de vivre*, *Cannery Row* is Steinbeck's high-spirited tribute to his native California.

Sweet Thursday

In Monterey, on the California coast, Sweet Thursday is the day after Lousy Wednesday, one of those days which is just bad from the start. But Sweet Thursday is sunny and clear, a day when anything can happen. Returning to the scene of *Cannery Row*, Steinbeck brilliantly creates its bawdy, high-spirited world, telling the story of what happened to everyone after the war. There are colourful characters old and new, all united by love, laughter and tears: Fauna, the latest madam at the Bear Flag brothel, Doc, still there for everyone else but feeling strangely sad himself, and Suzy, the new hustler in town who might be just the girl to save him.

BY THE SAME AUTHOR

Of Mice and Men

The compelling story of two outsiders striving to find their place in an unforgiving world. Drifters in search of work, George and his simple-minded friend Lennie, have nothing in the world except each other – and a dream that one day they will have some land of their own. Eventually they find work on a ranch in California's Salinas Valley, but their hopes are doomed as Lennie, struggling against extreme cruelty, misunderstanding and feelings of jealousy, becomes a victim of his own strength. Tackling universal themes: friendship and a shared vision, and giving voice to America's lonely and dispossessed, *Of Mice and Men* has proved one of Steinbeck's most popular works.

The Long Valley

These short stories, written over several years and first published together in 1938, are set in Steinbeck's birthplace, the rolling Salinas Valley in California, a land of farms, ranches, sunny hills and distant mountains. Haunting and acutely observed, they explore the tensions between men and women, the individual and society, and humanity and the natural world. They include the chilling, prize-winning tale 'The Murder'; 'The Chrysanthemums', possibly his most ambitious story; the gritty lynch mob violence of 'The Vigilante'; and the classic 'Red Pony' tales. In these works Steinbeck developed new ways of storytelling, honing the artistry from which his great novels would emerge.

To a God Unknown

With his father's reluctant blessing, Joseph Wayne leaves the family home in Vermont and travels West to fulfil his dream of creating a prosperous farm. Settling in an idyllic Californian valley, Joseph comes to believe that a magnificent tree that hangs over his new house embodies his father's spirit. Joseph invites his brothers and their families to join him and the farm flourishes. Then one brother, frightened by what he thinks are Joseph's pagan beliefs, destroys the tree ...

BY THE SAME AUTHOR

The Grapes of Wrath

'I've done my damndest to rip a reader's nerves to rags, I don't want him satisfied'. Shocking and controversial when it was first published in 1939, Steinbeck's Pulitzer prize-winning epic, *The Grapes of Wrath*, remains his undisputed masterpiece. Set against the background of Dust Bowl Oklahoma and Californian migrant life, it tells of the Joad family, who, like thousands of others, are forced to travel west in search of the promised land. Their story is one of false hopes, thwarted desires and broken dreams, yet out of their suffering Steinbeck created a drama that is intensely human, yet majestic in its scale and moral vision; an eloquent tribute to the endurance and dignity of the human spirit.

East of Eden

'There is only one book to a man' Steinbeck wrote of *East of Eden*, his most ambitious novel. Set in the rich farmland of Salinas Valley, California, this powerful, often brutal, novel follows the intertwined destinies of two families – the Trasks and the Hamiltons – whose generations helplessly re-enact the fall of Adam and Eve and the poisonous rivalry of Cain and Abel. Here Steinbeck created some of his most memorable characters and explored his most enduring themes: the mystery of identity; the inexplicability of love, and the murderous consequences of love's absence.

Also published:

Burning Bright
Cup of Gold
In Dubious Battle
The Log from the Sea of Cortez
The Pastures of Heaven
The Short Reign of Pippin IV
Travels with Charley
The Wayward Bus